THE PROMISED LAND

a true fantasy

A NOVEL BY GRACE OGOT

the promised land

modern african LIBRARY

Published by
East African Publishing House, 1966
Uniafric House   Koinange Street
P.O. Box 30571   Nairobi, Kenya

Printed in letterpress by
East African Institute Press Ltd.
Saldanha Lane   P.O. Box 30502
Nairobi, Kenya

for
my beloved husband
BETHWELL ALLAN OGOT

1

The fierce tropical thunderstorm was over. But far away towards the lake flashes of lightning could still be seen as the rain poured down. It was bitterly cold; the coldness which everyone expects during the wet season. The wind blew furiously, as if it wanted to shake the little huts free from the earth. The village of Owiti Kisero, the son of Opala, stood alone in the thick bush facing the River Awach, the boundary between the clans of Kombewa and Katieno. Torrents of water rushed down from the hills on the Katieno side, sweeping the rich red soil along and flooding the river below till it burst its banks.

Although the fire was still burning, the hut was cold. Near the stones enclosing the fireplace, some rainwater had seeped through. It formed a dark ring on the wall.

Nyapol raised her head and listened. She thought she heard someone coming. But it was the wind whistling shrilly above the trees like a human being. Nyapol suddenly felt frightened and lonely. Her two bridesmaids, who had stayed with her for the first few weeks, had just left. Before her marriage Nyapol had never felt loneliness. Her father had many wives and she had many step-sisters. They had all slept in their grandmother's hut and talked and laughed together well into the night.

But, in this last week, loneliness had begun to creep in. How could she exist in this isolated village? There was not a single woman of her own age — her only companions were three old women. Two were Ochola's step-mothers, the other was a relative who lived with them. Nyapol threw a few more sticks on the fire. It did not need them but she had to do something. Her mother had always said, "If you're frightened don't sit still, keep on doing something. The act of doing will give you back courage." She walked over to the bed and took out her wooden comb and head scarf from under the pillow. Her hair had been plaited only that morning, but she would drive away the loneliness by doing it again.

As Nyapol thought of her two bridesmaids who had returned to their home in Nyahera that morning, tears came to her eyes. Abonyo had been her closest friend since childhood. They had grown up together, sharing their secret joys and sorrows. Abonyo was only six months older than Nyapol but she was tall and well-built. She was a strong girl with a sweet, musical voice that rang out in the night when she laughed or told stories of the olden days. Nyapol had come to depend on her as she would on an elder sister. Once, when Nyapol's betrothal to Ochola reached breaking point,

Abonyo had saved it. She stood firm and trustworthy as if God sent her from Heaven specially to negotiate with stubborn relatives.

The betrothal had started well but bogged down in the middle, as if evil spirits were jealous of seeing human beings so happy. Ochola and his relatives had visited Nyapol's home twice, bringing four cows and five goats. But on the third visit, when they had brought two more cows, the women had deliberately abused Ochola's people. They had suddenly discovered that Ochola was not handsome enough to marry their beautiful daughter. He must therefore pay compensation for his ugliness, extra cows on top of the usual dowry. Ochola was furious. He had never thought himself ugly and if he was, certainly no one had ever told him so. To hear it from women! And women who were to be his relatives!

Ochola's people were supposed to stay the night to rest their blistered feet and to give Ochola a chance to talk to Nyapol alone for a few minutes, beyond the inquisitive eyes of the in-laws. But they left for Seme that evening.

While a group of girls accompanied the visitors as they left the village, Nyapol and Ochola kept a little behind. They said nothing. The sudden crisis had taken them by surprise, leaving them helpless and confused. When a small bush hid them from the others, Ochola grabbed Nyapol hungrily and crushed her to him. Then he pushed her roughly away and faced her.

"Tell me quickly why you stabbed me in the back! Your mothers could not speak like that unless they have some one else in their minds for you. Nyapol, listen! No one shall take you away from me. Tell your mothers so. How can you put a calabash of water to my lips and suddenly remove it,

9

leaving me to die of thirst? Night after night, I thirst for you, like the cracked sun-baked clay soil thirsts for rain."

Nyapol opened her mouth to speak but Ochola put his right hand over it, and stopped her.

"Don't say anything to me until you have quenched my thirst. Why must I suffer injustice all my life at the hands of hypocrites who claim to know what is right for me? This time I must win. I shall win — I shall have what truly belongs to me."

Ochola looked up the path. The others were waiting for them. They hurried to catch them up. The girls could not walk any further with the guests — they had reached the end of their clan's land, and it was dangerous for them to go further. Ochola and his friends reluctantly bade them farewell.

Nyapol remembered the rest of the story clearly. That night she had wept and refused food until her mother assured her, out of her father's hearing, that she herself had nothing against Ochola and that she deplored the behaviour of the other women. She had known many unworthy men marrying girls from their clan, without the women behaving in such a manner.

On their return the girls had assembled in their grandmother's hut. They had talked, laughed and told stories well into the night. But even when the others did eventually sleep, Nyapol remained awake. She closed her eyes tightly and the warm, salty tears ran down her right arm, with which she was supporting her head, and dribbled on to the mat. The secret Ochola had made her keep smouldered in her flesh. The sensation she felt when Ochola crushed her to his chest was still alive in her young erected breasts. The warm blood rushed through her until her whole body seemed to be boiling. She opened her eyes and mouth and breathed deeply, but the feeling remained. She trembled with fear. Yes, this was the secret Ochola would not let her tell. Nyapol had not yet known a man and the burning fire within her could only be extinguished by a man she loved. She lay praying and longing for what she had not yet known. It was well after midnight when the burning fire died down. At last she slept.

Nyapol's thoughts were interrupted by a strange noise — she listened; yes, there it was again. A chill ran through her, paralysing her movements. She fumbled with the fire-wood and threw more sticks on the fire, but now she felt very frightened. Then she heard the mooing calves running loose in the cow-pen. She herself had tied the calves on the pegs outside her hut when Ochola had finished the milking. It could only be a wild animal or a thief that had let them loose.

The fear left her, but bitterness and resentfulness stung her heart until she cried. It must have been midnight already and Ochola was not yet home. He had murmured something about going out for a few minutes. His food was still covered up on a small table away from the fireplace. Nyapol was furious that Ochola could leave her alone for such a long time while she was still a mere bride. Perhaps she would leave the calves to find their mothers. But people would blame her the following morning. She was no longer a child! The women had told her so on the day of her marriage. Moreover, there were hundreds of wives whose husbands were away earning money in the town, while they were left to fend for themselves in lonely isolated villages.

11

She gathered courage and rushed out to see what was there. All the pegs were empty. The calves were loose and had run back to their mothers in the cattle pen. She moved swiftly amongst the cows, found the first calf, dragged it towards the hut, and tied its leg tighter than before. She started back to look for the second calf, but as she bent to catch it, a harsh voice startled her. " Who is there? Stop or I will kill you!"

Nyapol let the calf go and stood stock still, facing a man who held a raised spear.

"Who is it?" the voice demanded again. This time Nyapol recognised her husband.

"Who did you expect to be here at such an hour?" she answered, her own voice trembling and tears blinding her. She reached again for the calf.

"What are you doing alone in the cow-pen at such an hour?" retorted Ochola.

Instead of replying, she dragged the second calf away from its mother and tied it roughly on to a peg. Resentment still filled her heart and she refused to look in her husband's direction.

Back in the hut she warmed the fish quickly and put it back on the table. The *kuon* was cold and stiff.

"Just leave the dishes on the table," she said. "I will see to them in the morning."

She was not really sleepy; she wanted to go and sit near Ochola and ask him where he had been all this time. But her anger told her it was better to go to bed.

The small oil lamp flickered on the table, while steam from the fish curled its way weakly up to the roof. Though Ochola looked steadily at the little oil lamp before him, his heart was not there. He felt guilty that he had stayed away so long while his wife was still a bride. But the proud voice of a man inside him said, "What's wrong in a man staying out as long as he wants?" He had built Nyapol a good hut and furnished it well. If she wanted to sleep early, what prevented her? Waking up once in a while to open the door for a late-coming husband was part of a wife's duty. Of course he did not like the idea of her running out in the cow-pen chasing the calves — he ought to have been at home to do that. But to apologize now would be to set a precedent and then each time he came home late, he would have to explain where he had been.

He was not hungry. He had eaten at Ochwonyo's home, where a group had gone to meet some visitors from Tanganyika. But fearing to offend his wife a second time, he ate some of the *kuon* and fish and covered the dishes again carefully. Then he sat still for a long time. The bed creaked as Nyapol moved, interrupting his thoughts. He got up and undressed. As he crept into the bed beside his wife, she pretended to be snoring and talking in her sleep. She had made up her mind not to respond to him, come what may. But to her chagrin Ochola turned his back on her and continued to be preoccupied with his own thoughts.

He thought of the conversation he and his friends had had with Ochwonyo's visitors from Tanganyika. He was convinced that what the visitors had told them was true. He was already imagining that he was in Tanganyika, where the land was fertile. He knew that there were many Luo people from Nyanza living there. Many of them had made their

13

fortunes. They owned large farms of maize and millet, beans and vegetables and were producing quantities of milk and ghee.

Ochwonyo's visitors had said that wide expanses of the land were virgin territory. You could take as many acres as you could cultivate. He was getting tired of living in Nyanza, with its unscrupulous tax collectors, its petty tyrants and its land feuds. Whatever money anyone could make went on school fees, hospital fees and so forth. Sub-chiefs regularly recruited forced labour to work on public projects. Why were people made to pay tax as well, then? He pondered the beauty of Tanganyika in his mind. Perhaps people did not even pay taxes there? The heavy sleep of early morning overpowered him.

Nyapol woke early. She cleaned the dishes and started preparing breakfast. Ochola lingered in bed a while before getting up to milk the cows. When he returned with the milk, he put it in an off-hand manner near the fire-place inside and sat at the doorway gazing at the dark clouds. When Nyapol called him inside for breakfast, he refused to join her and asked for his food to be taken out to him. Nyapol ate her porridge quietly near the fire place. She cleared the things, swept the room and left the homestead for the shamba. Ochola watched her go — he did not even call her to wait for him as he usually did. When Nyapol had gone, he washed, changed and went to Ochwonyo's home to talk again with the visitors from Tanganyika.

"How did you actually move to Tanganyika?" asked Ochola.

"Well," said one of the visitors. "I just decided that I was tired of living in Seme, packed up my things and left.

Same with Lanya here, he joined me a year later. He has been in Musoma for only two years, and he can tell you for himself how he is living."

Lanya sat smiling — he was expensively dressed, his hair was brushed back and he wore a gold ring on his right finger. His jacket, patched with brown leather at each elbow, made him look very important. Ochola felt awkward before them both, and the feeling irritated him. He was poorly dressed because he did not have enough money. The men were obviously telling him, indirectly, that he was a fool not to go to Tanganyika and make his fortune, while he was still young and energetic.

"I am interested in migrating to Tanganyika one day," Ochola told them at last. "Most of our land is washed away by the floods each year and the yield is not as good as it used to be. Indeed the only thing that prevents me is the old man."

"What is wrong with the old man?" the visitor asked, laughing.

"Well, he is all right but he is too old now to look after the other members of the family, so I stay around to help him."

"Haven't you got a brother or someone else to care for the family? By going away you will become rich and be able to send enough money for the old man to live as luxuriously as a chief. What about your brother Abiero?"

"Oh, he is working in town — he comes home now and then, but only for a short time."

"But the old men are changing with the times too. When I went away, my father protested but now he says I did the

15

right thing. I bring them bags of maize and gallons of ghee regularly. If he was not opposed to sailing, he would have visited me by now."

"I shall definitely take your advice seriously," Ochola told him.

Ochwonyo's wife put some tea before them. Other people kept coming in from the neighbouring villages to see the visitors from Musoma.

The sun was high in the sky when Ochola at last joined his wife in their garden on the slopes of the Otiato Hills. Nyapol continued to weed. She did not even look in her husband's direction. Ochola started to weed his strip from where he had left off the day before. He did not speak, but worked furiously to make up for the time he had spent at Ochwonyo's home.

The visitors from Tanganyika had left no doubt in his mind that he had to move. But it was going to be hard for the old man — that he knew. His brother Abiero, who regarded him as his right hand, was not going to like it either. He stood up to rest his back. The land of the Kowe people sloped steeply from the top of the hill to the river below. Strips of tidily weeded land revealed the life-giving red earth, while the green plants bowed in one direction to worship the midday wind. Little had changed since he had first accompanied his mother to weed this same garden. That was nearly twenty years ago. Then he had been too short to see the acres and acres of land that now lay before him. Twenty years, a very long time, but as far as he could remember, nothing had changed. The little round villages, surrounded with euphorbia fences, stood between the strips of land where people eked out a living.

Why had God been sleeping for so long? When he created this land, he must have had a better purpose for it. He must have said that this land, like the land of Canaan, would flow with milk and honey so that its inhabitants could have plenty to eat and drink and live a better life. Yet Seme was no Canaan, and there was no hope that the land would ever be fertile like the cows whose udders are full of milk even during the dry season. The land that stretched before Ochola was a tired land which had nourished maize and millet crops since time immemorial. The exhausted soil had no rest from the wretched little hoes that scratched its surface only to make it easier for the floods to sweep up the good soil.

Ochola caught Nyapol's eyes on him and he bent to his hoe again. Perhaps God was not sleeping, but was merely watching the wisdom of man. He made the land, yes, but He had given it to man. If a man was a fool, he would toil foolishly, reaping but little each year until he, man, according to God's word, returned to dust. Ochola caught up with his wife. The strip of land that he was cultivating was narrower than hers. He tried to start a conversation, but Nyapol was in no mood to talk. She was upset at his behaviour the night before and his mysterious disappearance after breakfast. It was late in the afternoon before they went home for lunch. Nyapol walked some distance apart from Ochola, deliberately avoiding him.

During the weeks that followed, Ochola had no peace in his mind. The things that he had previously loved in life now meant little to him. The burden of making a final decision weighed on his heart till he lost all sense of time and place and neglected his wife in a way she had never known. For a time Nyapol ignored him but, towards the end of the third month, they had their first bitter quarrel. Nyapol tried to be patient and she did her best to obey the customs by treating everything with a smile, but things grew worse and worse. The Ochola she knew, the man she had once loved so dearly, had disappeared. He ate little and spoke to no one. He lost the enthusiasm for work that had so struck Nyapol before she had married him. He stood for long periods with a hoe in his hand, day dreaming. At night he tossed restlessly in bed, snatching a few hours of sleep before dawn. Small things irritated him quickly and he had become dissatisfied with the beautiful hut which he had built with such pride. Sometimes he was so touchy that he refused even to taste food.

Nyapol thought herself cheated. She was still the most beautiful woman in the entire village and its neighbourhood. Her beauty was still far above that of Ochola's cousins who were not yet married. The tiny mirror she possessed did not flatter her. Everybody in the neighbourhood said she was beautiful. Any mother whose daughter looked attractive would say, "Oh what a lovely little girl you are. If you grow up to be as beautiful as Nyapol, the daughter of Kisumu, I shall have many cows."

Nyapol wondered sadly what had turned Ochola against her so much. She cleared the dishes from the table and instead of washing them up she put them in a basket near the fire-place. She too grew moody and refused to talk. She washed her feet, threw out the water and crept into bed. Ochola remained smoking and staring into nothing. Nyapol gripped the hard pillow tightly under her head — her heart was sore and the desire to have a child burned within her womb. She had failed to start a baby for two months running. She had been hoping she might be lucky this month. But Ochola had been cold and indifferent, ignoring her and making no advances. What kind of a woman did he think she was? The way he was going on, perhaps he was thinking that she should make advances to him! He would be a fool to think that! She started sobbing and talking to herself. If Ochola ignored her, she would do something drastic. To her surprise, Ochola suddenly jumped to his feet and went to her. He put his arms round her and asked tenderly, "What bothers you? Have you received bad news from your home?" The grip of his hand temporarily calmed Nyapol. The warm blood rushing along her veins made her heart beat faster, bringing back old memories of her wedding day.

"I have no bad news from home." She started sobbing loudly.

"Then what is it, Daughter of the Rulers?" Ochola's voice was hoarse with emotion.

"You treat me as if you only picked me up from the market place. What have I done to the ancestors to deserve such cruelty? You don't eat the food I put before you. You don't talk to me and at night you forget that I am a woman longing to hold a baby in my arms."

Nyapol's voice trailed away in a whisper but Ochola heard her. His grip around her tightened. Her words had shocked him and he felt ashamed of himself.

"But it is nothing to do with you, my pretty one." He leant his head towards her till his lips touched her ears.

19

"Then what is it? If you're already tired of me, let me go free so that I may return to my people."

But she knew very well that she could not return to her people. Once a woman was married she swore to stay with her husband's people for better or for worse, and no one would have her back at their home.

"I have been wanting to talk to you for a long time but I have been waiting for the right moment. Now I feel bad you have taken my mood so seriously."

"You must tell me now. I must know. You tell me that you care for me and yet you keep things hidden from me. You make me suffer loneliness as if I were an orphan who had no one to talk to. Have you forgotten the happiness of my home, Ochola?"

"All right, I will tell you everything," he said, at last.

He let her go and undressed. Throwing his clothes carelessly on to a chair he lay down beside his wife. He wiped her tears with his hands, and ran his finger through her hair. She kept still, waiting. The thought that perhaps Ochola's old father was not satisfied with her and that the family was having second thoughts about their marriage made her tremble, and she waited for Ochola to speak. He lay quietly, wishing he had not kept his secret for so long. Now the subject had come up in the wrong way. He had intended to break the news to his wife when she was in high spirits but Nyapol was already annoyed with him.

"Do you know Ochwonyo the son of Rabare?" he said, after a long silence.

"Yes," Nyapol answered slowly, her anxiety moving away from the old man.

"Well, a short time ago, some visitors came to see him from Tanganyika," Ochola continued. "They are some of our people who migrated there many years ago to farm the land on the slopes of the River Mara. They also trade in cattle and ghee. These visitors told us of the beauty and wealth of that land and the enormous yield they get from the crops each year. Since that time I've been thinking..."

"But what has that to do with us?" said Nyapol. "Tanganyika is so far away from here. You couldn't be thinking of opening trade with them?"

"I wasn't thinking of starting trade. I've been thinking we might migrate there. I would work very hard, become rich and make you happy."

Nyapol pushed Ochola's hands off her hair and sat upright in bed.

"You must be talking in your sleep!" she cried. "How can you think of such a thing! Leave Nyanza! Leave our old parents to go and live in a foreign land because some unbalanced men with no love of their families have told you so?"

She fell back on the bed, faced the wall and sobbed loudly. Ochola put his arms around her, but she pushed him away.

"I don't want to hear any more — I don't want to have nightmares."

Ochola lay beside his wife, thinking. He could hear the careful snoring of the calves safely tethered on the pegs

21

outside his hut. It was wise to keep quiet now until his wife had recovered from the first shock. Nyapol sobbed herself to sleep.

The sun was not yet up. Nyapol struggled to keep her eyes open. She had a splitting headache and her throat was dry and sore. She lingered in bed for a while. Had Ochola really said something about going to Tanganyika the night before? Perhaps not? Perhaps he had just been joking, or pulling her leg, to see how she reacted to things. But if that was the case, he was taking his jokes too far.

Ochola had woken earlier, put the milk on the table, covered it, and left the house. Thinking that he had gone to the main village, Nyapol pulled herself out of bed and prepared breakfast. She set it on the table and waited but Ochola was still nowhere to be seen. She looked in the cow-pen — he was not there. Then she discovered that his hoe was missing.

She put their breakfast in a basket, took her hoe and left the village. The sun was up now, but the morning dew was still thick on each blade of the long grass. The countryside was peaceful except for the hungry birds which sang noisily from the trees. The homesteads across the river rose out of the earth, resembling the brown, poisonous mushrooms that children are forbidden to touch. The small plots of cultivated land were green with the young millet and maize plants which had now almost passed the weeding stage.

"How could anyone think of leaving this land? Our ancestors died fighting for this land. The Nandi lived in these valleys and on these hills and they drank from the river below. The land was fertile, but the Nandi did not cultivate the land — they were herdsmen. Our grandfathers

22

declared war on them because they did not know the
value of land — they grew no crops or vegetables. The
battle raged for two full market days, and afterwards many
warriors were never even buried. They were drowned by
the angry river in the depth of the lake. The Nandi were
driven away to the mountains."

Nyapol had not seen the battle, of course, but her
father-in-law had told her the story.

She soon arrived in the field — it did not seem as
far as usual as she had so much to think about. Ochola had
weeded a longish strip and she felt proud of him. He threw
down his hoe and joined her under a sycamore tree to eat his
breakfast.

"You don't tell anybody when you come to work," she
said, avoiding his eyes because she loved him.

"I assumed you were still sleeping," he answered.
"Anyway give me some porridge. I'm starving!"

"I thought you were at home and so I put some out for
you on the table. When I didn't see you, I thought that you
didn't want any," she said teasing him.

"Who? Me? I can't miss my breakfast," he said. He
drank a mouthful. "Mm, this porridge is good."

"I'm glad," she smiled.

Ochola was unusually friendly and Nyapol wondered
what he had up his sleeve — it was good anyway to make up
for the past sad weeks. They finished the porridge and
started to drink their tea in silence. Neither of them spoke.
Above them, on the branches under which they sat, a solitary

dove sang endlessly, its lonely lament sounding for all the world as if it were mourning for a lost lover.

Far away across the River Awach came the throbbing sounds of drums — and the shrill voices of women and girls. A change of wind brought the sound nearer.

"Can you hear the drums and voices?" Ochola asked his wife.

"Yes, they started at cockcrow."

"I wonder who has died?"

"Maybe it is Opiyo's mother — she's been ill for a long time. The voices seem to be coming from their home."

"That would be sad," Ochola said sorrowfully. "It is the wrong time to have a funeral. The granaries are already empty and buying food for mourners at this time is as difficult as paying dowry for a wife!"

Nyapol piled the empty utensils in the basket and made a gesture as if to start weeding. But Ochola asked her to wait.

"I'm sorry you were so upset last night," he said.

"I am still upset now," she answered firmly, feeling sad that Ochola was reopening a healing wound.

"There was no need to be upset. Many of our people who have moved to Tanganyika have made a future there. The men I spoke to were very rich. It's a pity I didn't take you to Ochwonyo's house for you to see them yourself. You would now be feeling just as excited as I am."

Nyapol threw down her hoe and sat on the protruding root of the tree under which they were having breakfast.

"Please let me get this clear. What are you trying to tell me? I can't follow."

"There is nothing to explain. All I've been telling you since last night is that we're going to move to Tanganyika and settle there as soon as we agree on the date."

"Who are 'we'?" She eyed her husband from head to toe, tears burning her eyes.

"You and me obviously — I've only one wife."

"I'm not moving anywhere! Do you hear me?"

Nyapol rose to her feet, threatening him with her fingers, a thing she had been told never to do to a husband even when she was annoyed.

"We're rich as we are and we've enough land. Instead of working hard on the land which belongs to us, you make arrangements behind my back to move me from my people, to make me a beggar in a foreign land."

"What have we got to be called rich? Sit down and stop pointing at your husband with your finger. Do your women do that in your home? And remember, I hate being interrupted when I'm talking. There can only be one husband in the house. I'm making all these difficult decisions in order to make you happy. I'm telling you a very important matter and you don't want to listen. When I do it without informing you, you weep because you are not consulted. Women! Useless the world over!"

"You're abusing me for nothing," Nyapol cried covering her face. "I was just trying to say that now there are two of us, we can produce more than enough food for us to live on."

25

But Ochola cut her short.

"Now that we are two, we can make the narrow strips of land wider. Is that what you're trying to say?"

"Rich, rich, every man wants to be rich," she was weeping loudly. "It's all greed. Greed killed Okal Tako. This is the fate of men who want to get rich too quickly."

Nyapol felt better now she had let off steam.

"We're not risking our lives," Ochola emphasized, and returned to his hoe.

"You are," she replied, following him. "You'll disappear there as the rest of them have done. People who go to Tanganyika never come back."

"Well, you'll see to it that I don't disappear there like the others."

"I'm not coming with you," she nagged.

"You *are* coming with me. When I married you, you promised to obey me."

"I don't want to be a stranger among strangers," she persisted stubbornly.

"Well, I advise you not to mope about it any more and no more nagging. It's all decided."

Now Ochola in his turn eyed his wife from head to toe in the way that a short man might look at an opponent who was too big for him to fight. He bent again to his work.

Nyapol blew her nose, wiped her tears and started weeding blindly, accidentally felling a large nearby ripe maize plant to the ground.

The family gathered to hear about Ochola's decision to migrate to Tanganyika. Abiero came with his wife. They had received the news from a neighbour who claimed to have heard that Ochola had already packed up his belongings. Owiti's distant brothers and some of the old men who were members of the clan had also come to see them.

The men sat in front of Owiti's hut. Some were smoking, others were chewing tobacco. The women sat in front of Ayo's hut, a short distance from the old man's, where they could hear the proceedings. The cows were not yet back home, and the sun had not started descending to the west. On arrival the visitors accepted a drink before they discussed the extraordinary news.

29

"Put your words before us, my son," one of the old men said to Ochola.

Owiti felt so ashamed that his son had let the news leak out to neighbours before telling him, that he let the others speak first.

"There is not much to say, Grandfather — I am just thinking of moving to Tanganyika. I want to live there, like so many of our people have done," said Ochola.

"Son, we heard this and thought it must be an idle rumour. Do you now tell us, to our faces, that you want to leave your home to be a stranger in Tanganyika, amongst foreigners? You must be mad, my son."

"I'm not mad, my Grandfather. I've told you what I want to do. I'm an adult and I hope you'll take me seriously and respect my views."

"But how can we leave father alone?" Abiero chimed in. "He's an old man and I'm away in the town. How will he manage? I could understand it if you were going to work in Tanganyika, leaving Nyar Nam behind. But to migrate for ever. . ."

Ochola did not comment. Abiero was only a young boy. He had done his best as an elder brother to build a home and to keep the old man company. Kisumu was only a day's journey from Katieno. If he was such a good father's son, why could he not come home once a month, to make sure the old man was all right?

"Would you take Nyapol with you?" another old man asked.

"Can a hunter go to the wilderness without his spear, my father? Can you go to cut wood without an axe? I cannot go to Tanganyika empty-handed."

"But what drives you away from here? You've enough land at the moment, and when your father sleeps, being the first son, you'll inherit all his as well. It is better for a man to live with his relatives. The strangers, amongst whom you want to live, may not be good people. They may be unfriendly and you may not find favour among them. You know the fate of the strangers who live amongst us here? They have no voice in the running of our land. They're lonely because they're not accepted by our people. Is this what you want? You who are descended from a distinguished clan? All your grandfathers were warriors. They died fighting for this land. Why go away and be destitute, leaving your inheritance here?"

The family conference continued until the sun disappeared. But there was no agreement. Ochola retained his ground. He had made up his mind to go. Nyapol was weeping in front of the old men, afraid that she and Ochola were going to waste their lives. The meeting broke up and the old men went their separate ways. Abiero stayed behind to have dinner with his brother and the old man, in the hope that Ochola might still change his mind.

"You might at least listen to your father," Nyapol told Ochola in tears, when the visitors had gone.

"I'm a married man now," Ochola told her angrily. "It is high time I was given a chance to plan my own future and to provide for my family. Father should agree to give me this chance."

31

Owiti was peace loving. As a young man he had fought in several clan wars and was fast with his spear. Now in old age he went about with a long stick to steady his bent back and to give him confidence. His broad shoulders still showed traces of well-developed muscles, and his narrow, wrinkled face still revealed a touch of the handsomeness of his youth. Owiti wore no clothes, only a sheep's skin sewn up at the shoulders with the pieces hanging front and back, leaving both sides open. He had three wives. His first wife, Ochola's mother, was the daughter of a fisherman who lived in Uyoma near the Lake. After their marriage Achar bore her husband two sons; Ochola, the eldest, and Abiero. But fate was against Achar. She died young when Ochola was only ten years old, and Abiero was two years younger. She left him with two small sons and no one to look after the home.

After the days of purification and mourning, his brethren urged him to remarry. So Owiti took a young woman from his late wife's clan to be mother to his two children. But for the children, the new marriage was not a success. The newly married step-mother was unkind to them. She beat them, called them names, and made them work hard in the fields without food.

Often she shouted at them, "You don't want to work, but you eat like white ants. Why don't you dig up your lazy mother from the grave so that she can cook for you? I didn't come to cook for orphans."

Sometimes Owiti heard these outbursts, but he felt the loss of his wife so much that, instead of quarrelling, he walked away to find peace by herding his cattle on the plains. When his children told him of their sufferings, he simply bowed his head and wept.

But during the third year of Owiti's second marriage, the relatives stepped in and demanded that Owiti should marry yet another wife. They could no longer bear to see the way Achar's children were treated. They were weak and miserable and when no one was at home they wept beside their mother's grave. The women nearby often gave the children food but they did this privately, lest they incur the wrath of the step-mother. Under great pressure from the women, Owiti took a third wife, from Ugenya, near the River Nzoia.

Chila was not beautiful but she had gentle manners and a ready smile. She was plump, and her stiff breasts shook as she moved. The children liked her at once, even when she was a new bride and still confined to her hut. When Owiti asked her to care for them, she accepted readily saying, "They will stay with me till they are old enough to live in their own huts."

Chila turned a deaf ear to any abuse from her co-wife. She took the children into her hut and cared for them as if they were her own.

Under the love of the devoted Chila, the boys started life anew. They went with her to the fields and helped her at home to her heart's satisfaction. Ochola was maturing into a man and Chila allowed him to spend more time with his father in the evenings. Out of the hands of his jealous step-mother, he developed faster and became a good companion to his father. Owiti often spoke to him about the tribal traditions and the clan wars. Owiti knew the names of all the clan heroes, and taught Ochola to recite them. He had strong feelings against the changes that were undermining the old customs.

33

In a small way, Ochola was very much like his mother.
Though young he understood Owiti's simple life, and helped
him make many decisions, as Achar had done before she
died. And when Owiti's younger son, Abiero, went to school
and became a Christian, it was Ochola who mediated between
father and son.

Abiero changed. He became so possessed with his faith
that the villagers thought he was mad. He stole his father's
precious pipe and broke it on a rock outside the village.
He was hostile towards any of his younger step-brothers or
sisters who sang traditional songs. The teachers at school
had said that all these were sins, things of darkness.
Anybody entering the new life and starting to learn to read
and write should reject such things and abide by the big
books of wisdom.

Abiero took all the school teaching very seriously; even
dancing to the throbbing African drums annoyed him. Eager
to civilize his brothers and sisters, he sang Christian songs to
them with great fervour.

Owiti was greatly disturbed by this new faith. Abiero
now disobeyed him in many ways. But Ochola comforted
his father saying, "I am your first son and I have decided to
stay with you to listen to your voice. Abiero is just a child.
Let him learn the white man's secrets. We are no worse
off than Okelo, three of whose sons have gone to school."

Owiti listened to his son but asked him to watch his
younger brother lest he bring a curse to their home.

*　　　　　　*　　　　　　*

Nyapol brought food and set it before the old man. The hut was in semi-darkness and Nyapol could not see her father-in-law's eyes.

She murmured, "Please, father, persuade him, persuade him again. I don't want him to go!"

She wanted to say more, but at that moment Ochola appeared to join his father for supper, and Nyapol left them. At supper time father and son chose their words carefully, as if they were meeting for the first time. And when Nyapol collected the dishes, she noticed that Owiti's side of the *kuon* was only scratched, the old man had hardly eaten at all. They sat in silence for a while, then Owiti faced his son again.

"Son, don't go away, don't leave an old man alone," he began. "You brought this girl here to feed me. She's kind like your mother and her presence has given us all a new life. Let her stay with us, son. I ask you this favour."

"But I must go, father. I'll be more useful to you if I go," argued Ochola. "I'll be rich and all the money troubles we've had for so many years will vanish. Whatever I earn I'll share with the whole family."

"You are my eldest son — this land is yours. Our fathers died fighting for this land so that you might inherit it. It is the more precious because your grandfathers bought it with their own blood. Why go to a strange country to buy land? I'll soon lie in my grave. The land we have is more than enough for you, my son. You're married now, stay near me here. If you go away, who will bury me when I die?"

"I'm sorry, father, it's hard for you, I know. But I must go."

"Stay with me, son, don't leave me here alone."

"When I'm rich I shall come back to you. I'll bring you many things, but now poverty drives me away."

"Riches! I don't desire riches! I'm rich as I am! I live on our own land! But what I need most is your company. Don't deprive me of that my son, don't deprive me of that!"

"It's all arranged, Father. I must go."

They sat in silence for a long time. The oil lamp burnt out and they sat on in the darkness. The old man's heart was breaking with grief. He knew that his son would never come back home. Those who migrated to Tanganyika never came back. He could remember several sons of relatives who had never been seen or heard of since they had left. Tears ran down his cheeks, and on to his naked chest. He realised that he had always regarded this sort of thing as other parents' problems. Now he was faced with the same trouble right on his doorstep. For weeks the old man stayed in his hut weeping, and offering secret prayers to his dead wife to help him change their son's mind. The old man knew no more peaceful sleep, and his face grew more wrinkled than ever before.

But Owiti's prayers and entreaties were in vain. At the end of harvest that year, Ochola and his wife sold the whole crop. This time it was not for tax collectors, but for their steamer tickets across Lake Victoria to Tanganyika. Many visitors came to see them off. Nyapol's people came. Her mother and the other women brought new seeds and beans for her to take away. Her mother wept and the pain in her heart told her she would never set eyes on her daughter again. Tanganyika was so far away and once there, people disappeared. Nyapol's father and brothers came.

A cow was slaughtered and beer was brewed. The couple were blessed at a special ceremony before they left. Nyapol wore a sad expression for many weeks. But she was not alone. At times she caught Ochola too in a sad, thoughtful mood. He was becoming weighed down by the family opposition that had now rung in his ears for many weeks.

Ochola packed up all the things that they would need to start their new life. But the journey was long and they could not carry much heavy luggage. Some of the precious things that he inherited from his mother, he distributed amongst his family.

He gave one of his cows to his brother saying, "Son of my mother, take this cow and keep it, drink of it's milk. If it gives birth to a heifer, that will be yours. But if it gives birth to a bull, then keep it for me. Do this in memory of our mother."

Ochola's land, the two fertile strips lying on the banks of the River Awach, were left in the care of their kind step-mother who had given him a home after the death of Achar, his mother. In one of these farms he had planted good, healthy bananas and sugar cane.

"Mother, I leave all these in your care," Ochola said to her. "It was you who loved me and covered my nakedness and saved me from starvation. If it were not for you, I might have followed my mother to the grave. When the world turned against me, it was you who saved me, and because of you I am now a man."

Chila was weeping. She sniffed and spat on the ground. "You are breaking our hearts, a well-loved son leaving his home to go and live amongst strangers. Go, if you must, but come back in time to see your father before he sleeps with his forefathers."

The days soon passed away. The packing was finished. Ochola gave some of his furniture to his father, who refused to acknowledge the gift. Some he gave to his younger brother, Abiero, who had taken two weeks leave to be with his father after Ochola's departure.

The August moon was shining brightly. All was quiet. Everyone had gone to bed except for the old man whose hut was purposely left open. A small oil lamp threw a weak light on to the table on which it stood.

Ochola called to his wife. "The hour has come."

Together they left the hut. Nyapol carried newly harvested red millet in a tiny basket and simsim seed, mixed with beans, in a calabash. Ochola carried a small white cock under his left arm, and in his right hand he had a live fire. They stood at the foot of the *siala* tree, where lay their mother's grave. It was covered with grass and wild vegetables, which had grown up over the years, dropping their seeds for the next season. No one moved. Ochola was going against the tradition in leaving his home. If his dead mother was as displeased as his relatives, God would not bless them at all. Ochola lifted his eyes to heaven to communicate with the spirit of his mother.

He opened his mouth and whispered, "Hear me, mother! Wherever I wander here on earth, I shall never forget you. The memory of you, and the symbol of your grave, will abide with me, burning in my heart like a light and guiding me. In this village, where your spirit lives, will I lie when my time comes to join you. So hear my plea, mother! Ask

God, on my behalf, to bless me and my wife, and guide our feet to the unknown land."

Likewise Nyapol moved an inch forward. Her voice was trembling.

"Let God bless me through my husband's mother. I never knew you, but my heart is full of respect and love for you. See, I have brought you new food, red millet, simsim and beans. All the food that I reap during the harvest I share with you, my mother. Bless me with children, that your name may live with us forever."

Then she sprinkled the grains on the grave and stood silently for a few moments before stepping back to where Ochola was standing.

The shadow of the big tree partly covered the grave. There was no movement except for the cows chewing the cud in the cow-pen. Yet, as Ochola fixed his eyes on his mother's grave, it seemed to him as if the stones were saying to him, "Don't go, don't go. Stay with us, stay with us!"

Ochola touched his wife's shoulder.

"Go into the hut," he said, firmly.

She obeyed. Ochola lit the fire. Then he took the chicken, sprinkled it's blood westwards and put it over the fire. He went to his father's hut and called to him. They went out and sat near the fire until the chicken was roasted. Then they tore it apart with their hands and ate it. When they had finished, they threw the bones on the fire to burn, and the fumes purified the night.

*   *   *

Dawn was breaking. The family assembled in the yard to bid farewell to Ochola and his wife. The women were clad in their night clothes, and the children squatted naked in front of their huts. They did not understand why Ochola and his wife were going away. They could not imagine a country which was better than Seme. Seme, the land of their birth, where they drank plenty of milk and ate vegetables floating in ghee, who could want to leave it?

The family shook hands and stepped aside. The old man spoke to Nyapol and blessed her, but as he was her father-in-law, he could not hold her hands.

Owiti held his son's hand for a long time but instead of blessing him, he looked steadily into his eyes.

"I have no future to look forward to, and the present is fast closing itself before my eyes. All I can do now is leave you both in the hands of Him whose home is beyond the stars."

Owiti was old and weak and he knew that his days on earth were numbered.

"Son," he sighed, "you will not find me alive when you return, but remember your home. Remember your brother and your mother and remember these younger members of the family who will grow up without knowing you."

The family stood together and watched Ochola and his wife until they disappeared into the darkness. They were passing Omolo's deserted village. The long eucalyptus trees covered the air making the path completely dark. Ochola's heart was heavy, as though he was uncertain about the journey. He wished it was broad daylight so that he could see, perhaps for the last time, the land where he had lived all his life. He had followed this narrow path so many times and he knew each tree that lined it on either side.

"You'll have to walk faster than that, Nyapol, or we'll miss the bus," he said.

"I'm doing my best," she sulked. "If you want me to run, say so. I'm already feeling sick and the cold wind is entering my bones. I'll be lucky to reach Kisumu alive."

"You'll be all right, my pretty one," Ochola said in a softer voice. "Just keep going. We must catch the steamer today, or we'll have to wait another week."

He let her walk in front of him, talking to her and encouraging her as they went. It was important to catch the boat. Nyapol walked faster and Ochola praised her. The sky was much lighter now and the birds were waking up and singing to welcome the new day.

They arrived at Awach Junction. Several people were already waiting there, warming themselves in the morning sun. The Uyoma bus had not yet arrived, they were told. Uyoma was about thirty five miles from Awach junction and during the rainy season the roads were sometimes closed, owing to the soft, mud surface. The little bus stop hotel was open, and a man was serving travellers with tea. Ochola went in and bought two cups of hot tea and two slices of unbuttered bread. Nyapol was grateful and they ate in silence. The tea was rather too sweet and made her feel a little sick, but it warmed her up.

"Rest there and I'll stretch my feet by the river," said Ochola, when he had returned the cups. He lit his pipe and moved towards the bridge. The water was forcefully rushing towards the Lake, but Ochola looked at it without really seeing it. The idea of leaving his birth-place worried him much more than he would admit to his wife. Supposing that

41

the visitors from Tanganyika were lying? Was his wife right when she said that his move was motivated only by greed and the desire for money? If he found that there was no land to be had and the people were hostile, how could he face returning home to the people he was now deserting? How they would laugh at him and abuse him!

He could not find the answer. It was certainly not in the rushing water below the bridge. But the stubborness in his heart told him to go forward. "Don't look back, move on," it said. "If you retreat you'll be mocked as a coward." Standing there alone Ochola surveyed the land around him. The Katieno Hills stood out in the distance, kissing the delicate rays of the sun pouring in from the East.

Below the hills lay the beautiful valley, covered up by the blanket of morning mist. The entire country was peaceful and undisturbed. Ochola recalled what his father had told him about the bitter war between the people of Seme and Gem. It had occurred on the very land on which he now stood. Then the people of Gem wanted to drive the people of Seme to the steep hills, which today are occupied by the Banyore. But the Seme overpowered the people of Gem and killed many of their great warriors. The people of Seme retained their land, and were able to hand it over to their children. The land was beautiful and very fertile then, but now it was tired. He was right to move to new, untried pastures.

Ochola was still immersed in his thoughts when Nyapol shouted to him that the bus was coming. His heart pounded with excitement as he rushed back to collect their belongings. In no time the Uyoma-Kisumu bus appeared. It swerved and lurched dangerously to a standstill at the side of the road where the passengers were waiting. Within minutes their luggage had been thrown on top, while a bus conductor packed the passengers in a space hardly enough to seat a child. Nyapol started to grumble, but when she noticed the discomfort on the faces of the other passengers she kept quiet. Babies were screaming and some passengers were talking at the top of their voices and laughing. Cigarette smoke, children vomiting and the smell of humanity all combined to produce a stale sickening smell that choked Nyapol as soon as she entered the bus. A passenger complained bitterly that the bus was too full. The conductor turned promptly on him.

"You get out and walk," he said and shook his fist rudely. "What do you people want? If I leave some behind, because the bus is too full, you curse and swear at me. If I squeeze you all in, and save you waiting a whole day, you abuse me. Well, gentleman, you either get down and walk or keep your big mouth shut."

The man looked at the conductor in dismay and kept his mouth shut.

The packed bus groaned several times before it started moving. A blanket of smoke followed behind, saturating the air with diesel fumes. Nyapol glanced sadly at the village where she had been married and had lived for only a few months. She did not have many friends there, but she had become deeply attached to the old man and to her step-mother-in-law. She would also miss Nyariwo who plaited her long hair on Sundays. She knew the old man would miss her taking him his breakfast. Since her marriage, she had taken him a large mug of sweetened tea each morning, sometimes with boiled cassava, or sweet potatoes and, when they were lucky, a slice of bread.

Nyapol's thoughts were interrupted by a big jolt as the heavy bus bumped its way over the lower bridge, which consisted of boards precariously suspended on cement pillars. The jolt was a severe one. She felt a sharp pain in her womb, and tightened her lips. She cursed the driver and blamed Ochola for exposing her to such rough travelling during her early pregnancy. Yet the Government was partly to blame. They combed the villages turning people's purses inside out looking for taxes. But still the narrow bridges were washed away by the floods each season and the people themselves had to replace them.

The sun was bright when they arrived at Kisian Junction. Many passengers alighted from the bus to stretch their legs. The driver got out and blew his nose.

"Kisumu next stop," he said in a cheerful voice.

They were well ahead of time.

There was a warning whistle and the passengers scrambled back on board. Presently as they were passing through the Kisumu plains, the Lake stood before them. The ground seemed to slope, yet the water did not spill; the sunlight made it sparkle and the beauty of it was overwhelming. At the little pier small boats tossed about lazily in the morning wind. Beyond the boats, stood the the great s. s. "Rusinga", the giant of Lake Victoria which was to carry Ochola and his wife away to the unknown land. From time to time, thick black smoke puffed up from the steamer and, from a distance, it looked like a burning island.

Ochola turned to his wife excitedly. "Can you see that big ship at the pier head?"

Nyapol nodded, her mouth full of sour saliva.

"Can you imagine that within a short time we shall be aboard that giant and sailing away on the Lake? I'm sure you'll enjoy the journey."

"Let's hope the lake will be calm," Nyapol said slowly, with a sinking feeling in her stomach.

Ochola could not help feeling important. He had looked forward to this time ever since he was a boy. The day he would take his wife to town, as he had seen many of his clansmen do. It was a matter of great prestige in those days to go to town and be in contact with the new ideas and acquire the new ways of life. People living in towns obviously ate better food than those who lived in the country. They ate at regular hours too. Nyapol listened to her husband patiently; she wished she could be as excited as he was about the journey. There was so much she was going to lose by leaving Nyanza. Now and again she glanced at the hills of Nyahera and thought of her birthplace beyond.

She thought of her mother and sisters who were, perhaps, even now enjoying the tales of old times in the village they had lived for so many years. She wished she had not married. Marriage was a form of imprisonment in which the master could lead you where he wished. The bus reached the terminal and Ochola and his wife hurried to the pier, taking the lower road that passed across the railway bridge. There were many people walking towards the ship. Nyapol's heart cheered a little as she hastened her steps to the noises of the town. The lorries and cars frightened her, and she walked close to her husband.

They reached the big iron gate where they bought their tickets; each ticket cost nine shillings and seventy cents. They moved to the goods shed, a long building with a corrugated iron roof, originally used to store maize for shipment to Uganda and Tanganyika. It had no walls, just supporting pillars, so that Nyapol could see through it over the water. They found a place and sat down on the hard, wooden benches with the other waiting passengers.

Ochola sighed with relief. He was very excited and restless, but something stopped him showing his feelings. There was no need to show Nyapol that he, a man who had taken her as his wife, did not like his own motherland. Already some of Nyapol's remarks had made him feel as though he was a shallow-minded person without roots.

When they had quarrelled some nights ago, Nyapol had spat on the floor and told him, "There's nothing to be proud of, leaving your inheritance to go and live as a refugee amongst strangers. The Umuri people left their land and came to live in your land and now you won't even recognise them. You call them names and you look down on them. Why? Because they are foreigners who know quite well that they have no right to our land. Their fathers didn't conquer it like our fathers did. It's time you swallowed your pride and accepted the fact that you're a lost man."

Ochola was annoyed beyond words by Nyapol's speeches. No man had ever spoken to him like that, even those who thought they were stronger than he was. He had slapped her on the face twice because he was provoked beyond control. But Nyapol did not cry. She sat where she was as stubborn as a mule, as though nothing had happened. Perhaps Nyapol was right, Ochola thought bitterly, but how long it was taking her to learn that it was not correct to speak to a husband in that way! They had made it up later, though only after Nyapol had refused to talk to him for a whole day.

He glanced at his wife. He would not slap her now, even if she annoyed him. Her first pregnancy made her look more beautiful than ever and, in the morning sun, her brown olive skin shone like that of a young child. No wonder men glanced at her where she was sitting, looking out at the passers-by.

"To be walking with a pretty wife is like wearing a beautiful flower; it catches the eyes of travellers," thought Ochola, well pleased with himself.

"I'm hungry," he announced, to break the silence.

"Have you seen any food around, or shall we eat our own?" asked Nyapol.

"No, keep ours for the journey. I'll buy some tea from that canteen. Perhaps they have some buns too."

He went over to ask.

Nyapol looked at the steamer steadily. It was big, perhaps the biggest thing she had ever seen. It had windows and doors and stood very high out of the water. She was impressed. The only thing that frightened her was the gangway which was precariously suspended between the steamer and the dry land. It did not look safe. She had a worried feeling that it could collapse into the water while people were going on board.

Nyapol looked a little more relaxed after having tea and Ochola was happy to watch her. He would not talk to her much about the journey now, but when they arrived on the other side he would show her that in taking her away from the land she loved, he only meant to do well for her sake. He would be rich and give her all she had ever wanted. This would help her to forget the past.

The man sitting opposite them looked very anxious to talk to them. Perhaps he was feeling lonely, as his wife was busy feeding the baby. He exchanged greetings with Ochola and soon they were deep in a discussion which did not interest an expectant mother at all. Nyapol did not mind — she wanted to be quiet and to look at everything around her. A European woman passed by and stared at her. The woman looked beautiful. She had slender legs, and a long neck but the sickening smell that she left behind made Nyapol loathe her. Perhaps she was sick, her skin looked ghostly pale — like a baby that had been born before its time. How could her husband stand that smell? But wait a minute, come to think of it, she had sensed that queer smell before. Yes, when she was young and they had gone to confess their sins before Father Ellis — she could remember now. She had knelt down before him. "What sins have you committed this week, my child?" the Father had asked her repeatedly. But some peculiar smell from his body had suffocated her and made her violently sick. She rushed from the church without telling him her sins. Father Ellis had found her vomiting in the churchyard. Instead of telling him the truth she told him she felt ill. From that day onwards, she had never been to church.

Her younger sister had continued going to church every Sunday, but she never stayed long enough to be dipped in the water and to get a new name. One day she came home weeping bitterly. Their mother had not returned from the market, and Nyapol was busy grinding the millet on a stone near the fire-place.

"What's the matter?" she asked her anxiously.

"Just the time I've wasted," Apiyo wept.

"What time?" Nyapol was puzzled.

48

"I wanted so much to be baptised like the others, but now I have to give..."

"Don't behave like a child," Nyapol coaxed her. "What happened? Tell me quickly before mother comes."

"Father Ellis sent me away from the church," said Apiyo wiping her tears. "Because I bit his hand."

"What! Bit his hand?" Nyapol was both shocked and disgusted. The man was God's image on earth, and Apiyo had gone to tell him her sins, so that he could plead with God to forgive her. Moreover the holy man's skin smelled terribly. How could Apiyo bite him with her teeth?

"Why did you bite him? His God will punish you."

"Why did he squeeze my breasts? I'm not his wife! My breast is aching, look I am bruised!" Apiyo pulled her breasts from under her petticoat.

Nyapol looked at her sister's young breasts. She did not believe her at first, but the bruises were there, particularly on the right side. Her mind became confused. Ever since the White Father had come to the hills, the people were told that the white man was married to the service of his God. It was wrong to talk to a woman. It was a sin in the eyes of God. Now that Father Ellis had in fact squeezed Apiyo's breasts, the way other men do when they desire a woman, the women were bound to take him before the clan elders. He had defiled the girl, for what man would marry a girl who had been touched by a white man?

"Make sure you keep your mouth shut, Apiyo. You'll never get married if the boys know that the white man has touched you. Remember, I told you to leave that man's God alone, but you wouldn't listen to me."

49

Their mother appeared at the gate. Nyapol resumed her grinding, Apiyo pretended to be making the fire. For several days she tied a cloth around her chest to hide the bruises from her mother's searching eyes.

*   *   *

Ochola learned from his friend that the steamer had been delayed for two hours. It would now leave Kisumu at noon. He was most disappointed. Nyapol already looked bored and this was going to make her even more resentful. Such delays were bad omens, particularly when you had a long journey ahead. A pile of cargo had just arrived by goods train and had to be loaded before the steamer left Kisumu. He thought it wise not to tell his wife what had happened.

The wagon train stopped with a jolt and all eyes turned towards it. Within minutes, the wagon was surrounded by half naked men, some of whom had quickly climbed on to it.

Then a song broke out,
'*Harambe! ee!*
Harambee! ee!'

The men had not finished uttering the words when one man stepped forward and bent below the wagon, his friends whisked the bag load and rested it on his back lengthwise. The man trotted pitifully with the load, towards the steamer. He hesitated on the pavement, bent to one side and the bag fell to the ground. The man straightened his back and ran back to the wagon.

The song continued several times as the men tottered along with the bags, which looked bigger than themselves. The contents might have been maize, millet, or groundnuts,

each weighing up to two hundred pounds. Nyapol found it inconceivable that the same men she had watched trotting with heavy bags on their sweaty backs went back to the wagon laughing amongst themselves and grinning at the stupefied passengers. Once they were back at the wagon, they wasted no time before taking on another load. In fact, it looked as if they were competing to see who could carry the greatest number of bags.

It was not anger that made Nyapol's eyes sting with tears. It was pity. Though the men obviously looked happy and proud of their work she concluded that they had been bewitched — laughing under such conditions was lunacy.

When the men finally began to show signs of exhaustion, Nyapol lost her control and sat there, sobbing quietly. An hour must have passed. The sun was high in the sky and beat furiously upon the naked chests of the labourers. They were perspiring heavily and beads of sweat from their heads poured down their faces and mingled with those on their chest. Their worn out backs were white-washed with dust from the bags, while their once protruding bellies were now sunken.

"Why waste your tears? The men have chosen the job themselves. They are neither slaves nor prisoners: they are just normal men who have come to town to earn money to buy things for their wives," explained Ochola, seeing his wife looking at the labourers and weeping for them.

"Ridiculous! Only bewitched men could willingly choose such a job! A man whose wife is bewitched as well."

Ochola tried to explain to his wife about contract jobs but she would not try to understand. He was not in a mood to argue; he soon kept quiet and let his wife recover on her own.

Nyapol jumped as the giant steamer boomed a loud warning. She was so frightened that she stood up and gripped Ochola's hand. Ochola soothed her.

"That's the signal to tell us that we should go on board," he explained. "There will be another hooter to announce the departure of the steamer."

3

A crowd of passengers rushed on board. Women,
clutching children in their arms, were wriggling their way
forcefully along the gangway and frightened children
were screaming their heads off. Men, carrying heavy loads
on their heads, broke their way through the crowd,
pushing the women mercilessly in order to get on board
first. A mother, leading a small child, and with an enormous
load on her head, was making her way up the gangway.
A man wearing heavy army boots, came running up
from behind and pushed past her, crushing the little girl's
toes against the concrete pavement. The child wailed with
pain and bent to nurse her bleeding toes with both hands.
Nyapol looked at the man in terror. There was something
inhuman about his eyes — he did not look back at the child,
but forced his way on, until he managed to stagger aboard.

"Here's our chance to move. Let's take it or we'll be here for ever," said Ochola. Nyapol stepped on to the gangway and, as she started to move, a man rushed past her, nearly knocking her to the ground. Her husband saved her.

"You're not going to push past us, don't you realise that we want to go on board as well as you," shouted Ochola.

He barred the way and pushed Nyapol forward. The man shouted abusively but Ochola stood still.

"Keep moving," he whispered to his wife.

Then he followed her closely until they were safely on board.

Nyapol was shaken and puzzled. Things were so different in the town. Politeness was considered a weakness that these town people exploited. Everyone looked after themselves.

A sudden thought came to her. The white man was clever to be able to make such a big thing, and to enable it to keep afloat on the broad waters. Yet she was puzzled at the wisdom of the white man. Why could he not stand at the gate and say that only a few people at a time should walk up the gangway? That is what Ondijo did with his small boat, when he carried people across the River Awach during the rainy season. Indeed he was so strict that women and children were told to go on board first. Perhaps the white man was not so wise after all. The steamer was so huge that it could take all the passengers comfortably if only he had the ability to organise where they should go.

Within a short time Nyapol realised that you could not take your time going on to a white man's boat. You had to rush on board or you were left behind and the boat sailed away without you. They had not found a place to rest when they heard a scuffle on the pavement. Two savage-looking policemen stepped towards the gangway, pushing away the passengers who had not yet boarded the boat. By this time the steamer had hooted a second warning of its departure. It had to sail, even if all the passengers were not on board. The police shouted to the would-be passengers still left on the quay.

"You're too late now. You can't go on board. Why didn't you go on with the others?"

But the people did not listen to the policemen, they went wild with rage and several of them took hold of the two policemen and fought with them. Meanwhile, screaming women and children rushed on board. The gangway was so packed that no one dared lower it. A very fat European, wearing white uniform, descended from the other gangway. Within minutes, more policemen had arrived on the scene.

But the fighting was over, and within seconds, the rioters were halfway up the gangway. They were cursing, the policemen were cursing and the European jeered and shouted "bastards" at the men. The crowd of relatives and porters, who had gathered near the boat, moved back in fear of the police. The gangway was let down with a bang and the steamer set sail.

A wide strip of water now separated them from the dry land. The crowd of excited relatives at the pier looked smaller and grew increasingly blurred as they moved further and further away. The plains of Kano were spread out along the lake shore and the ragged Nyahera hills were still visible in the distance. Nyapol could just make out the direction of her home. Far away on the right the land of Seme gleamed, its rocky mountains kissing the sky. Ochola's long awaited dream was about to be fulfilled. They were leaving their motherland.

The third class section of the boat was open like a kraal. A few rough-hewn, hard, wooden seats were fixed here and there. People in third class were clearly not meant to sleep. Ochola found a small corner for his wife, and led her there.

"Sit down near me," Nyapol begged him.

He did so.

"Don't worry about me," she said.

"I just feel anxious that you may find the journey too tiring."

"No, we're together, so nothing can happen to me. Just pray that I don't feel sick. I hate the water," answered Nyapol bravely.

Not far away from them, a group of men were pleading with two musicians.

"Come, come and play for us," they were saying.

"Wait until the people are settled," the men shouted back. "It's no good playing for a few here and a few there."

"No," others begged them, "Sing something. Your golden voice will draw the crowd."

A tall middle aged man stepped forward — the people cleared a space for him. He tied bells on his ankles,

tightened the strings of his harp and played. The crowd
surged forward. An old man begged them to sit down and
they obeyed. The harpist then cleared his voice and sang a
wartime song.

'Listen, Sons of Ramogi, listen!
Listen, you who have been spared to live and eat!
They were young like you. They were fathers like you.
Some were engaged to be married.
But they had not felt the worth of a woman.
It was a day like this.
The sun was warm and the fields were red with millet.
The men were resting after the midday meal.
The women were nursing their babies.
The brides were ripe for marriage.

Then the hour struck.
It was the year 1939.
The chief's drum throbbed.
The people gathered and the chief spoke to them.
Hear, all of you, Sons of Ramogi.
The white man is at war with his brother across the seas.
Orders have been forced down my throat.
Let your people go across the seas to help me fight my
*   enemy.*
When I win the war, we shall divide the spoils.
His words were sweet and the chief's hands were forced.
He called the elders,
Let your sons go and help the white man.
When he wins the war let him give you half the spoils.
Bring them home.
We are brave people. We will fight.
So the men went to war across the seas to fight for
*   the white man.*

Opiyo went. Adhiambo was left behind heavy with a
    child, their first child.

Oigo went, he left a bride weeping.
Nyanyiwa went. He was strong and brave, he had paid
    dowry but his bride had not come to him.
Sigana went, his children clung to him weeping.
He soothed them, Papa will come home after the white
    man's war.

So they went, one man from each home.
It was a day like this, the sun was hot.
The fields were red with millet.
But they never came back.
The white man's battle swallowed them up.
The Kipande they had carried was returned — but they
    remained.

They remained in the land where there was no sunshine
    nor the warmth of a woman nor the cry of a child.

Sleep on, sons of the soil. Sleep on.
You were taken from us young and strong.
You were too young to sleep.
The earth had no shame to have swallowed your souls.
And to hide you from the warmth of the sun.
Weep with me you fathers. Weep with me you, whose
    brothers sleep.

Weep with me, mother, weep with me, mothers
Who long for the warmth of a man.
My clansmen have slept.
My brothers are no more.
The sun is warm.
The fields are red with millet.

The brides are ripe for marriage.
But you see them no more.

Sleep, sleep, sleep, sleep in the land of the white man . . .'

The harpist's voice died away. He sighed and wept as he played the last notes. The people wept with him. The second world war had just ended. The harpist had lost two brothers and a cousin in Burma. But he was not the only one who had lost relations in the white man's war. Hundreds of Luo men, who went to Burma to help the white man fight his enemy, never came back home. The families gathered at the camps, old men, women and children, to be given the identity cards found on the bodies of their dead relatives. The wives clutched the papers they could not read. How could they be sure that their men were really dead? So they kept on dreaming; dreaming that one day a miracle would happen and their menfolk would return. But there was no miracle, never. The men did not return. Neither did the white man keep his word to divide the spoils with the families of the men who died fighting for him.

Ochola was anxious about his wife. She would have to sit up the whole night. The journey was going to be four days and four nights. Nyapol needed rest. He found another small corner on the deck and made a little place for her to lie down. It was crowded with children, who were crying continuously.

They washed and ate. As it was not yet dark, they sat on the benches talking and smoking. The harpist had sung many songs, mostly about the war, and now people allowed him to rest. The ghostly, hissing sound of the steamer breaking through the water made Nyapol sick. She lay in a small corner, covered up with a thin blanket. Ochola sat close

61

to her, watching over their belongings. Even if he wanted
to sleep, the place was too small for two to lie down. Nyapol
tossed from side to side. The board on which she lay was
hard and her back ached. At first she comforted herself that
she would get some sleep as soon as her body relaxed. But
then she felt something biting her. Something was
crawling on her neck. She caught it and squashed it. The
sickly smell of bed bugs filled the place.

"There are bugs in this place!" Nyapol cried. "And
they'll get in our bedding. Oh! I hate bugs. I told you I was
better sitting down."

"Take it easy," Ochola soothed her. "Even those sitting
down will pick up the bugs, and carry them in their luggage.
This steamer is infested with bugs. People always complain
of them. You'll just have to try to forget them and snatch
some sleep."

She obeyed him and closed her eyes and relaxed her
body but she could not sleep. The bugs nibbled at her and
the stale smell from the lavatories wafted intermittently on
to the third class deck. At dawn she dragged herself stiffly
to her feet. They had arrived at Port Bell.

Ochola thought the land around Luzira was very fertile.
Up the hillsides, there were large clusters of banana fields
reaching as far as his eyes could see. For the first time, he
saw the red Kiganda bananas about which he had heard so
much. He longed to go inland to see what Buganda looked
like. Though the land looked green, it lacked the beauty of
Seme, his own land of hills and valleys, of many streams and
clear waters.

The morning was marred by the spectacle of the
Banyaruanda, in a single, long queue waiting to board the

steamer. They were scantily dressed with only coloured blankets round them, tied with a huge knot on their left shoulder. The women wore blankets tied with strings around the waist and a loose *suka* over their breasts. They were migrating to some distant country from a famine. They carried large bundles of assorted belongings, either threaded on strong cords, or tied up in blankets. The men and young boys carried long sticks, some women were carrying their belongings on their heads, as well as naked babies tied round their waist by a cloth.

The group segregated themselves from the rest of the passengers. They looked poor, ill and hungry. Yet there was something genuine in their way of life — perhaps it was the strong family ties so that if they had to migrate, the whole family moved together. Among them were some beautiful fair-skinned women with long necks, like the girls from Kanyada in South Nyanza. A pathetic, separate group of people, they no longer seemed to belong anywhere.

*   *   *   *

It was a cold windy night when the tired travellers reached their destination. At last they were in Tanganyika, in the very region where they hoped to settle! It had rained throughout the night, and a thick white mist still covered the land. It was impossible to see anything from the steamer. While they were waiting for the gangway to be lowered, Ochola's heart was throbbing with excitement. He was longing to disembark and explore the land of his dreams! For years he had heard about Musoma. His father had told him that, during the great migration of the Luo-speaking peoples from Sudan southwards, small bands of adventurous Luo had penetrated into the western part of Kenya, sweeping all before them. The Luo people who had settled around

Musoma, had inter-married with several alien tribes, particularly the Suba. For this reason, Ochola's attitude towards his future homeland was ambivalent. On the one hand he felt he was a complete stranger going to live in an unknown country amongst unknown people, on the other he regarded himself as a latter-day Luo migrant moving into an area which had already been conquered. He realised that he was getting anxious and worrying about the unknown, but he told himself that he must not look upset. Nyapol must not trace a sign of doubt or anxiety in his face.

With a faint smile playing on his lips, Ochola whispered to his wife, "Look cheerful! We're here at last."

Nyapol's mouth was too full of bitter saliva to answer. She swallowed, and ignoring Ochola's assurance she cried, "When shall we get out of this smelly steamer? I'm sick of seeing water, water, water, everywhere. Get me out of here."

She buried her head in her hands to hide her eyes from the water.

As the thick mist cleared and the sun started to shine, the gangway was fixed and the excited passengers streamed ashore. Ochola carried most of their belongings on his head. Nyapol carried the small raffia basket in which they had packed the remains of their food. She picked her way very carefully, not once did her right hand leave the rail which was attached to the narrow gangway. She smiled when Ochola said to her, "Remember the Nyarwanda woman." This was an accident that had happened at Mwanza. An elderly Nyarwanda lady had missed a step on the gangway. She had slipped and fallen over on to the ground, knocking down all the other passengers who were in front of her. The poor lady lost her belongings but she was lucky not to be badly hurt.

Two men were waiting to meet Ochola and his wife at Musoma when they arrived. One of them was an elderly man who had lived in Musoma for many years. Okech, the son of Sipul, was like a father to the Luo people who had migrated to this part of Tanganyika. He had met and welcomed almost all those who had arrived after him. He was tall and strong. He was also wealthy and generous. He kept open house and made room for most of the new arrivals until they had found a place of their own. He greeted the travellers with open arms, as though he had known them all his life. Nyapol relaxed. Her feet were still numb but she was grateful to be on dry land once again.

Seeing that Nyapol was pregnant, Okech said gently to her, "You'll soon be able to sit down and rest. My wife will be delighted to see you."

Several people were waiting at Okech's village to welcome the visitors. They were all Nyanza people, except one Swahili woman who was a friend of the family. Okech's village was large and well cared for. There were several fat calves grazing near the gate. A big semi-permanent house stood at the far end of the village; on each side of it stood two small huts; a kitchen, a shed for the goats and calves. Everywhere in the home there were hens and their chicks pecking on the ground. The grass had been cut, and the village was swept clean. The shy, naked children peered at the strangers from behind the granaries. Perhaps they were wondering how long these new-comers were going to stay.

Okech's wife Nyaboro, better known to her friends as Atiga (a woman whose neck is as long as a giraffe's) was a most tolerant person.

She gave Nyapol a warm friendly welcome saying, "You belong here. God has brought you home."

These were the most comforting words that Nyapol had ever heard from another woman.

After bathing, the tired visitors relaxed and enjoyed a feast that had been prepared for them. The men drank some home-made beer, after which they quietly left for their homes. In the evening Nyapol stayed at home while Okech went out to show Ochola the land. They walked for about half a mile before reaching Okech's farm. The fields were all red with millet, and the maize was drying. Large beans, which had not yet been picked, lay on the ground. Ochola was dumb-founded. He recalled a sermon that a toothless old Church leader had once preached at Sunday school; how God had led the children of Israel to the land of plenty, the land full of manna and honey. To Ochola, Tanganyika was the 'Promised Land'.

He lifted his eyes to survey the area. On the spot where he stood, the black loamy soil looked very fertile. A few yards away from him was the River Mara, flowing gently towards Lake Victoria. On the river bank several cows were grazing: they were fat, clean and heavy with milk. Ochola had never seen such fat cows before. Beyond the river, on the opposite side, lay a thick forest, known as 'No Man's Land', where there were plenty of wild animals and wild fruit. Yes, it was all like a dream...

Lost in thought and staggered by the beauty of the country, Ochola whispered aloud, "Yes, this is my Canaan, this is my 'Promised Land'. There will never be another land like this for me."

The sun was rapidly sinking behind the irregular hill masses and it was getting dark. They hurried home in silence. Ochola had nothing to say: his dream had come true.

Dinner was served early. Many visitors had come to take food with the guests. The men ate alone at a large table, while the women sat by at a low table near the fire-place. They spoke in low voices punctuated with quiet laughter.

Many people praised Atiga and told Okech what a good wife he had. In spite of having had six children, she was slim with slender features and she had a sweet voice and tender ways which made Okech treat her gently.

The conversation would have continued late into the night, but Okech asked his friends to let the visitors retire early.

"They're here to stay," he announced. "We can talk to them another day."

So their friends left and Ochola and his wife went to the visitors' house, which had been built opposite the cattle-pen.

They talked for a few minutes and then Nyapol slept. The bed was comfortable and the night was warm, but Ochola could not sleep. His mind went back to Seme, his motherland. He could picture his old father, still grief-stricken at his departure. He recalled his mother's grave under the *siala* tree. As his thoughts lingered on the grave stones, a shadow seemed to move towards him and stood in the corner of the dark room. The shadow slowly turned into the image of his mother. He closed his eyes tightly but the image remained.

He covered his face with a blanket, but the image would not go. Then he burst into tears.

"What message have you for me, mother? You have blessed me, I know. You've brought me away from the land of my birth where, year after year, people quarrel over land. You've set my feet on this vast land so that I may inherit it. But you are not here without a purpose, mother. Instil the spirit of a man in me so that I may work hard and be prosperous".

At last the cold image of his long dead mother disappeared as quietly as it had come. Ochola moved closer to his wife, put his arms round her, and slept.

Nyapol woke up first. The room was already flooded with light. Ochola was still snoring. Nyapol stayed where she was lest she should wake him. She felt much refreshed. In fact she had slept without turning over once. She wanted to sleep on, but she fought the lazy feeling. It was not fair to expect others to wait on her. Atiga had spoilt her on their arrival the previous evening. She had had a good sleep, and now she must get up and help prepare breakfast. She crept out of bed, leaving Ochola asleep.

"Good morning, but why are you up so early?" Atiga demanded.

"I've had enough sleep. Can't you see the sun is already up? I've been sitting too much in that smelly steamer. I need some work to stretch my limbs."

Nyapol yawned and stretched her arms in the air.

"Nonsense," Atiga laughed. "You'll need at least a week before you're rested well enough to work. I don't know what it is, but something in that steamer drains the life out of a person."

Nyapol wanted to tell her there and then that she did not feel in the mood for work, but she kept quiet. Even if she was tired, she could not expect to sit around while Atiga cooked the food and brought it to her. The woman had six children herself, as well as a house full of visitors. She needed someone to help her.

Okech and Ochola ate their breakfast under the tree near the maize granary. Nyapol insisted on going with Atiga to the river, which was not far away from the homestead. They were passing through the shamba that Okech and Ochola had seen the evening before. The land was fertile and Nyapol looked in amazement at the large maize cobs that were already drying for the harvest. The field was very long; it stretched from the gate to the river bank. It was not the custom to say to Atiga's face that she had never seen such large maize cobs in her life, so she merely praised the fertility of the land.

The vast space lay before them. Beyond the river was a thick forest with tall trees. On each side the land extended as far as the eye could see, until it joined the blue sky. Nyapol already felt she loved Tanganyika and her heart softened towards her husband. Of course it was tragic to leave their people, particularly the old man whom she had promised to look after as long as he lived. But Chila was there and she was kind. "If we can send back money regularly, they can buy sugar and tea," said Nyapol to herself. "Chila would take care of the old man. What is important is to remind Ochola to return home now and again and see the family."

They arrived at the river. Atiga offered to fill their water pots. The water was clear and little white stones could be seen sparkling on the bottom. Fragile-looking tadpoles waggled their tails lazily in the shallows, drifting down-stream with the flow of the current.

"Do people bathe in this water?" Nyapol said, breaking the silence.

"Sometimes," replied Atiga. "But most people in this land wash at home. I've only seen children bathing down here, but as a rule, I don't allow my children to bathe in the river. With this thick bush it's not at all safe."

"It's better to bathe at home," said Nyapol, supporting her. "It's very embarrassing to go to the river for water and to find men bathing just where you want to fill the pots."

"Our men do it sometimes, but it's a bad thing," Atiga sighed. "Nor should women bathe in public."

She helped Nyapol to put her water pot on her head and they walked slowly home.

Okech and Ochola left home to explore the land again. This time they followed the path on the left, leading towards the plain. They walked for about a mile before they saw a small village perched on top of a hill. The house was made of red mud and the roof of old red tiles. The area was covered with thick grass and short bushes, and the land was hardly cultivated at all.

"Is that one of our people?" Ochola asked his host.

"No, that home has been there for many years. The owner belongs to the Nyamwezi people, who migrated from the north quite a long time ago. He's an old man. He keeps to himself and doesn't visit his neighbours. There's no proper road leading to his village, so people don't visit him much."

"He doesn't seem to have cultivated any land. What does he eat?"

"I suppose he lives on rice which he can buy from the shop. He owns quite a number of cows, and I hear he supplies the Indian shop-keepers with milk and ghee. I think he gets his food in return."

"What do you think of this area?" Okech said, stopping abruptly. They were standing on high ground facing the river. The fields were covered with soft, wild grass of the kind used for thatching. The red soil looked rich right up to the top of the hill.

"All this is virgin land," continued Okech.

"I'm very impressed," Ochola said slowly.

"The place is ideal for a home," said Okech. "Of course it's a bit lonely, but as you can see, most people here live alone. This is all farm land and people can't live grouped together. If you're interested in this area, it would make a great farm."

They explored further on, until they came to the wooden bridge over the river. They crossed this and walked about a mile into the forest. The land was still fertile, but it looked damp and unhealthy, so they returned to the river and followed the path going in the opposite direction. They walked in a wide circle of valleys and hills, but they did not see anything to compare with the land they had seen on the slopes of the hills facing the bridge. So they decided to return.

Okech told Ochola to pluck a handful of grass. He did so.

"Make it into a ring," he ordered.

Ochola obeyed.

"Now put it on the ground and put a sizeable stone over it," he went on.

Ochola did as Okech told him. Suddenly the meaning of these actions came to him. As a boy he had done this on several occasions when he had discovered a carpet of young mushrooms in the fields. Traditionally, if you made a ring of grass and placed a stone on the area, those mushrooms were not touched by anybody else. But Ochola had never thought that it could be the same with land. In Seme, land was passed down from father to son. This was too good to be true.

"This is no man's land," Okech told him. "You are the first man to put a ring of grass over it, so it's yours."

They stood for a while in silence, then turned away and walked home. Ochola trembled with excitement, but at the same time he was also afraid of something that he could not explain. The land was so vast and so fertile. Could it all belong to him? He walked a bit faster to catch up with his friend. Okech noticed that Ochola was impressed beyond words, and he felt proud that he had helped to make him feel that way. He had settled so many people on the land around the hills and each one of them had been successful. They were all grateful to him. Of course he did not expect any payment or reward for his advice because these were his people. A man who did not love his people was an enemy of the tribe.

Food was waiting for them when they got home. Ochola told his wife about the land and the site they had chosen for building: he promised to take her to see it when the sun went down.

Three weeks had gone by, and Ochola and his wife felt rested after the strenuous months of decision and preparation for their migration. They had seen a wide area of the land, and they loved all they saw. Nyapol and Atiga were sitting in front of the fire-place. Okech and Ochola were sipping tea after supper. The children slept.

"Son of Sipul, you have shown great kindness to us," said Ochola. "We say that a visitor is noble only when he stays for two days, but we have already stayed with you for twenty-two! Let me now build a hut for myself and my wife, while the soil is still wet and it's easy to dig the foundations."

Okech was quiet for a while: then he spoke.

"Our home is open to you and your wife, my brother,

and you can stay as long as you like. But I can read your mind. You don't cook two cocks in one pot, and I can't blame you for feeling that the pot is too small for both of us."

He paused, then faced Ochola again.

"When were you thinking of starting to build?"

"Well, tomorrow morning would be a good time, now that we have talked about it," answered Ochola.

"God will look after you," Okech told him. "He has blessed all of us, and you are no exception."

At bed-time, Nyapol told her husband that she thought it was the right time to move. She could not tell him so in front of Atiga who had cared for them so lovingly, and it was not right to speak up when her husband was talking. There were many uncertainties, but faith was with them, and the presence of someone more powerful was close to them. That night when Nyapol was sleeping, Okech called Ochola to come outside. Ochola was half expecting this. He crept out quietly to join Okech in the yard. The night was cool and the white clouds rushed across the sky, darkening the surface of the moon.

"My brother," Okech addressed him, "let not sleep overpower you in the early hours of the morning. You've a great task before you when the sun comes up. Call me when you're ready. I'll be awake."

"I will remember," Ochola told him, and returned to bed. Okech stood in place of a father to Ochola. The old man would have used those very words if Ochola had been going to put up a new home.

At the first cock-crow, Ochola woke up with a start. Nyapol was still fast asleep. He crept out of bed quickly and started dressing. All was still as he walked towards the door. Suddenly he felt that he must wake up his wife and tell her he was going. He must tell her she had to stay in the house in Okech's village, but he wanted her thoughts to go with him. He shook her gently.

"Wake up. I'm going now," he whispered.

Nyapol understood. She sat up in bed, looking at her husband; she knew she could not go with him.

"Go in peace," she said quietly.

Ochola left the hut, closing the door behind him. His wife stared at the closed door. Outside Okech stood waiting. Ochola was surprised to find him already there. They did not greet each other with words, but Okech handed him an axe, a panga, a big white cock and a live coal in a broken pot. Okech clutched the axe and the fire in his left hand, and took a panga in his right. The two men looked at one another for a long moment. Okech walked ahead to open the gate.

Nyapol sat up in bed, listening. Suddenly her ears pricked up like a watchdog's. She heard the gate open and close. Then she heard Okech walk back and close his own door, and she thought perhaps she ought to go and lock it. However, she was not afraid, so she did not get up. Her husband was out in the cold facing the loneliness of the early hours. The animals would be looking for their last chance of food before returning to their hiding-places. She would not lock the door. She wanted to share his loneliness. The sleep had vanished from her eyes and she lay there thinking.

The morning was chilly. It had not rained the previous night but the long grass was wet with morning dew. Ochola's feet felt cold as he walked along the bushy path. His heart was beating faster than usual. Was it because he was in a strange land? Putting up a new home should not make his heart beat so fast! He remembered a time when he was a boy. His father had woken him up at dawn one morning. He had jumped up from his sleeping place and wrapped a loin cloth round himself. Then his father had handed him a cock and a piece of live fire and told him to follow him. He did so without question till they reached a place chosen for their new home.

His father had said to him, "When you become a man you will have to build a home of your own. This is how you must do it."

Ochola was young at that time, but he kept his father's teaching buried in his heart.

The clouds covering the sunrise were red, with streaks of golden lines. Ochola looked hopefully for the sun, but it was too early for it to appear. He walked blindly on, until he came parallel to the little village standing alone in the bush on the slopes of the hill. The village looked like a ruin, yet Okech had told him that someone lived there. Then courage filled his heart, he was not afraid of the loneliness and vastness any more.

"If that man can live there alone, surely I can. There is no need to be afraid," he said to himself.

It was light when Ochola reached the place where he intended to build. The grass ring, with the stone on top, stood where he had left it. It was covered with dew. He made straight for the coop where he had left the cock the night before. He shook it. The cock was still alive. That was good. He pulled pieces of dry wood out of his pocket and placed them on the fire. Presently, weak smoke started to drift towards the sky.

When the first rays of the sun appeared, the cock crew a second time, then it settled down to rest. The sound echoed in the air, breaking the silence of the forest. Ochola started digging the holes for the poles of his hut. The wood had been cut and the grass dried. He was only going to build a small hut at first, but he had to finish it before sunset. Ochola worked energetically, and by eight o'clock the circle of holes sketched out the shape of the hut on the ground.

In the middle of the morning Okech arrived with two friends. Nyapol walked behind them carrying a basket of food for breakfast. The fire was still burning, and the cock was covered up in its coop under a tree near the building site. Each man was carrying building tools. They exchanged greetings and, while Ochola was having breakfast, they started working on the holes, deepening them enough for the foundations of the hut.

Nyapol stood by. The place looked very lonely and dangerous. It suddenly came to her that it would have been wiser to build a home close to Okech's village. The land was empty — they could live near each other and still have enough space. Should she tell Ochola her thoughts? No, it was too late! The foundations of the new house had been laid and soon the wooden poles would be in place. To say a word at this time might cause doubt in his mind and some misfortune might occur. Ochola would blame her for life. So Nyapol kept her doubts to herself and stood watching the men planting the pillars in the soil and then ramming them fast with stones and soil.

79

Nyapol spent a weary day. It was harvest time. The maize and millet were not quite ready but the beans were dry and people rushed to pick them before they burst open in the heat of the sun. Her secret doubts made her feel uneasy about their new home. Nor did she feel able to take Atiga into her confidence. In the early hours of the afternoon they went to Atiga's home to bring more food to the men. At a distance they could see the new hut gleaming; the roof had been thatched. Nyapol's heart leapt when they neared the hut. The thatching grass had been tied all round the walls and Ochola was levelling the floor. Okech was tying up the wooden door and making the shutter so that the hut could be locked up.

Nyapol gazed from the doorway. Ochola stood up with a jembe in his hand and smiled at her wearily.

"You must be collapsing," she said. "I can hardly believe what I see. This morning there was nothing here, and now I am standing at the doorway of my own hut!"

"Are you pleased?" asked Ochola proudly.

"I'm both pleased and amazed at the amount of work you can do." Nyapol smiled happily.

"Atiga tells me that I can't sleep with you here tonight," said Nyapol.

"Why should Atiga say that?" asked Ochola, in a hurt way. "You know it already. You've known from childhood that a woman doesn't sleep in a new home the first night after it has been built."

"Of course, I know that, but now we're not in our own country, I thought that the customs could be waived. I would like to keep you company tonight and this place looks so lonely," she said.

Ochola looked at his wife affectionately.

"Tomorrow night, yes, but not tonight," he said firmly. "What makes you think that people must abandon their traditions when they go to a foreign land? Don't you know that our ancestors' eyes follow us everywhere? You break the law today, or tomorrow, their eyes can see you. A month may pass, even a full year, but in the end you're punished because you've gone against the taboos of the tribe."

Nyapol saw the point and apologised. Like the God of Father Ellis, the ancestors' hands did not spare anybody who broke the law of society. Her mother had told her so on many occasions.

Before sunset, Ochola's work was completed. He made up his bed, and lit the fire in his new hut for the first time. He was to spend the night alone. The white cock was his only companion.

The night was unusually noisy, the crickets' chirruping was louder than usual and Nyapol could even hear the cows chewing the cud in the cattle-pen. She closed her eyes tightly, but ghostly images of wild animals bothered her. Sometimes she thought a voice told her that her husband had been attacked by wild animals. She turned from side to side until the first cock crew, then she dozed for an hour or so. In the morning she got up with a splitting headache.

Ochola returned to Okech's home in the morning to fetch his wife and move their belongings to their new home. He could not tell what happened to him, but somehow he felt older and braver than before. The night he had spent alone in the wilderness amidst the howling of wild animals had instilled some power into him.

Nyapol was relieved to see her husband. She concealed
the nightmares of the previous night and told him she
had not been afraid. In the same way, Ochola told her
that he had had a good night, and did not tell her about the
endless laughter of the hyenas that had almost paralyzed
him with fear. Okech and his wife brought some gifts for
their friends to start their new life and that afternoon they
moved their belongings to their new home. They were now
part of Tanganyika, the land they had compared with Canaan
on their arrival. The hut was damp all round and Ochola and
his wife had to keep a fire burning most of the time,
especially at night. Since the walls consisted of dried grass
tied tightly round the wooden skeleton of the hut they also
had to watch the fire carefully.

By evening Ochola was exhausted. They had an early
supper, washed, and retired to bed. It was a very cold
night, one that Nyapol was to remember for the rest of
her life. It was not so much the coldness, but the hyenas
that howled all around till dawn, and the weird
human sounding cries of the birds of the forest. The cries
penetrated her whole being and made the hair on her skin
stand upright. The more she covered her ears the more
closely she heard the birds singing:—

Kirumba, Kirumba
I am dying naked,
Adongo please clothe me.

Nyapol woke up sick with fear, her nerves on edge.

"Do you intend staying in this place or are we
moving back to Okech's village?" she asked Ochola timidly.

Ochola looked at her with hostility and did not answer
immediately. This was a matter on which he had to

82

stand firm, otherwise all his plans would collapse and they would never settle in Tanganyika.

He was a man! Nyapol knew that and she must know that every man however small, or however cowardly, must have a home of his own as soon as he had a family to support. What did she mean? He cleared his throat and faced her.

"What a question to ask. Only yesterday you said you were proud of me for having worked so hard in building this hut. Now our home is hardly a day old, and you ask me if I intend to stay here. I've no answer to give you." To avoid quarrelling Nyapol did not reply.

The problem of wild animals also bothered Ochola, but he did not admit to his wife that he was afraid. He could not betray the secret of manhood in the eyes of a woman. But he erected a strong, thorny fence all round his house and set up a heavy wooden gate that he locked at sunset. At night, he kept a big fire burning outside to keep the wild animals away.

Christmas was approaching and Ochola had built another more permanent, three bed-roomed rectangular house. It was made of thick mud with a thatched roof. The grass used for thatching was of a special kind, handled only by expert thatchers. Such houses stayed in good condition for many years and this kind of roof kept houses cool during the hot season and warm during the cold rainy nights. The floor was beaten hard and smeared smooth with a special soil mixed with cow dung.

Ochola and Nyapol moved into their permanent house without ceremony, because it was very near the time for their baby to be born. The rooms were spacious and light. Nyapol realized how lucky she was. Very few women in her age group lived in a beautiful house like this. In fact she felt it was not wrong to think that she was the luckiest woman in the world, although she knew it would be wrong to boast or to express her secret feelings to others. Bad spirits lived everywhere and they could do much harm. But Nyapol felt too happy to keep quiet.

"I've never lived in such a beautiful house before," she told her husband one day.

Ochola smiled without answering because he was deeply touched.

The couple received many things from their neighbours to start their new life; sheep, goats, chickens and different sorts of grain. The Luo people are generous with gifts towards visitors, particularly if the visitor happens to be one of their own clansmen. Afterwards they were expected to fend for themselves. Ochola and his wife received these gifts warmly, and in return entertained their guests generously. So the news of their arrival and subsequent settlement spread gradually to all their tribesmen who had arrived in the land before them.

Through the help of Okech's son, Madika, Ochola wrote his first letter home to his brother, Abiero. Ochola had never written a letter before. He could not read or write and he was embarrassed by the idea of asking people to write for him. Abiero, his brother, could read and write. He was amongst the first batch of boys who had rebelled against their parents and attended the white man's schools. Ochola loved his father and feared offending him. In those days, boys who went to school found difficulty in persuading women to marry them. Stories went around that those who went to school grew cunning like the white man. They were slack in daily community work and liked things to be done for them. This made them lazy husbands who could not be relied upon to protect their family and tribe from enemies. But that was many years ago. People who had been educated were now becoming richer and richer: those who could read and write had advantages over their friends who were illiterate. Ochola could not ignore the magic of sending a message to friends by means of making marks on a piece of paper.

He cleared his throat hesitantly. It was difficult to know what to say first. "Start now," he said to the boy whom he had engaged to write the letter for him.

The boy bent over the paper and waited for Ochola to dictate.

"To my brother Abiero," Ochola began,

"I should like to tell you that I have arrived safely in the land of Tanganyika. This land is very beautiful. It has many hills and valleys like the land of Seme, and the soil is very fertile. The soil ranges from light loam to heavy clay. There is a very high rainfall. A wide area near our home is covered with thick bush consisting of broad-leaved trees and long grasses. I have fenced in a large area of land for myself. Very few people live here, and those who do are mostly our people. I hope to plough a wide area next season. I should like to know how our father's health is. Tell him not to worry. Tell him that I shan't forget my home. Nyapol is well. She is busy planting vegetables at the back of the house, as we don't want to buy from others anything we can grow ourselves. Now I have no more words. If you get this letter, please reply.

> Good-bye,
>> From,
>>> Your brother,
>>>> Ochola."

Ochola sat back and listened to Madika read over slowly what he had written. He nodded, all the time wondering at the miracle of school education. When Madika had finished, he nodded in final approval. The letter was put in an envelope and the stamp affixed. Ochola posted it himself in the small local post office, three miles from his new house.

The sufferings of an orphan child had taught Ochola how to work hard. The long hours he had spent in the fields as a boy, taught him that he could only eat by sweat and toil. But the sufferings of those days had also left a bitter tinge of determination in his heart. There were so many children in the land, why was it that God took his mother away from him so early, while other boys had more than they deserved throughout their life? Some boys of his age group had laughed at him when he cried for his mother, while others despised him and called him a poor destitute. Ochola fought whoever despised him openly, but sometimes he prayed that bad luck would befall those boys who were unkind to him.

Ochola's ambition in life was to be rich. Richer than those whom he had known in his youth. He wanted to be rich like Polo, his step-grandfather, who had countless heads of cattle. Sitting alone near the house, Ochola planned out his work in detail. What kind of seeds to plant, how many cattle to start dairy-farming, and how to make the chicken houses. He had no capital to start all these things yet, but there was no harm in planning what he wanted. Okech had told him that he had some savings in the post office. There was no need to be shy, he would ask to borrow a small sum which he would pay back the next season. Nyapol startled Ochola from his thoughts. She came and stood shyly at his side. Her face was sad and withdrawn and her muscles tight with pain. Ochola jumped to his feet and looked at his wife.

"What is it, my dear one? You look ill," he said kindly. He put his arm round her shoulders.

Nyapol did not move but looked away from him.

"I am not ill," she said, weakly. "But I want you to call Atiga for me before the sun sets. I've been feeling unwell since yesterday, but it's nothing to worry about."

She had hardly finished speaking when she fell down in a faint. Ochola carried her to her bed. Then he hurried off to call the midwife. He ran almost all the way, reaching Okech's house in record time. Atiga sensed that there was an emergency and did not ask any questions. She packed her bag and gave instructions to the children to tell their father that she might not come back until the following morning. She hurried to the house with Ochola. Neither spoke. Within half an hour they were at Ochola's home and Atiga was at Nyapol's side. Ochola went out into the yard to milk the two cows that Okech had given him. He stayed in the cattle pen for a long time, not wanting to enter the house. He milked one cow but was too nervous to milk the second, and allowed the calf to stay with its mother. He had lost his own mother when he was only a child. Relatives had told him that his mother had died from severe bleeding after a miscarriage. Ochola was too upset to inquire into the details of his mother's death but, when he grew up, he always associated pregnancy with sorrow and death. So when Nyapol had announced to him that she was two months with child, Ochola received the news coldly, and refrained from discussing the subject that had tortured him since childhood. Now that Nyapol was in labour, numerous uncertainties crossed his mind, threatening him with disaster.

He closed his eyes, and tried to picture his mother's image. In the past this had been a great source of strength to him. But he could not see her to-day. Was she angry with him for having left the old man alone? He closed his eyes again, but no image of his mother came before him. At last he decided to take a walk towards the river; the sun was setting, but it was still quite light. He walked aimlessly until he reached the river bank. The water was flowing peacefully towards the plains and the serenity of the scene assured him that there was no danger. He turned round and walked slowly back. When he reached his house it was dark. He closed the gate and walked to the door. The shrill cry of an infant filled the air. His heart almost stopped beating as he entered the house and the yelling continued. The sitting room was quite dark. Ochola heard Atiga's voice and then Nyapol's, weaker, in the background. The infant stopped yelling. Although there were four chairs in the sitting room, Ochola stayed standing.

Presently Atiga emerged from the bedroom beaming with joy.

"It's a boy," she said and disappeared into the bedroom again without even commenting on Nyapol's condition.

Ochola rested his hands on the table and sat down on the nearest chair. He was longing to enter the bedroom, but was not allowed, until the midwife had cleared up and told him he could go in. He sat nervously scratching the floor with his toes until Atiga went into the kitchen to cook the supper. Then he went in to see his wife. She hid her face from him because her heart was torn apart with joy. The new baby was sleeping beside her. Ochola pressed Nyapol's hands in his. A big burden seemed to fall off his chest, leaving him feeling light and dizzy. He wanted to sing and shout, and to say many tender things to his beloved wife. But there were so many bad spirits about that it was too early to be sure that all would be well.

In the morning the parents gave their son the name which Nyapol had heard in a dream in the night. They called him 'Safari', which means journey, because Nyapol had travelled so far when she was expecting him.

*　　　*　　　*　　　*

One day, as Ochola was walking home from a visit to friends living on the other side of the hill, he took a wrong turning and suddenly came to the gate of the half-hidden village which he had noticed soon after his arrival in Tanganyika. The sun was still up and it was not yet milking time, so Ochola thought he would call and find out who lived there.

"Who knows," he said aloud to himself. "The man may be needing company, but is too shy to take the initiative. Nyapol needs more women's company, and if they are good people, we can visit each other frequently." Thinking thus, Ochola turned in at the gate.

The compound was heavily fenced with thorns. The gate was so narrow and low that Ochola wondered if the occupants entered by some other way. He stood for a while, wondering if he should wriggle inside. He made up his mind, having come all this way, that he might as well go through with it. Perhaps someone had seen him standing there, and he did not want stories to be started about him. He climbed through the gate and entered the compound. A woman was pounding rice on a wooden mortar in the yard. She was very small and thin. Her dark complexion was coarse and her short hair was plaited in numerous furrows with tails pointing upwards at the nape of her neck. A small ring of brass shone in her nose, a multi-coloured *suka* was tied above her breasts, leaving her shoulders bare.

She was obviously startled to see Ochola walking towards her. She threw the wood down and went quickly to meet him.

"What do you want?" she asked urgently. "Are you lost? Who are you looking for?"

Numbness ran along Ochola's spine and he stood motionless. The woman, seeing that he was frightened, forced a dry smile.

"Don't tremble, nobody will harm you, just tell me who you are looking for," she said.

"I just happened to be passing this way," said Ochola apologetically. "I'm a new-comer to Tanganyika. My village is down there near the river." He pointed towards his house. "I've been meaning to come and introduce myself. It's sometimes lonely here and we need company."

The small lady gave him another dry smile and offered him a chair.

"I'll call my husband," she said.

But before she had finished the sentence, an old man emerged from a tiny hut which stood alone at the far end of

the village. He walked briskly past his wife and stood facing
Ochola. He was wearing a whitish *kanzu* with short
sleeves and had a small black cap perched on his head.
He was very tall and thin, his dry skin resembling that of an
alligator. He had an unkempt beard reaching up to the hair
at the side of his head. His thin lips did not entirely cover
his protruding teeth and his small eyes were red and
unfriendly, giving him the look of a disturbed buffalo. His
long nails were bent inwards like the claws of an eagle,
and while he eyed Ochola curiously, several large snakes
wriggled out of the little hut from which he had come a
few minutes earlier. The snakes slithered up to him and
twisted round his legs.

Ochola mustered his strength. It was embarrassing
to tremble openly when a woman stood looking on. His
great grandfather Ochola, whose name he bore, was a
great warrior. This stranger was only a man like himself.
He would not run, he would stand there and see it through,
come what may. At a sign from the old man, the snakes
returned to the hut. Ochola could hear his heart beating
louder and louder. He counted the beats. The old man took
advantage of Ochola's terror and asked in a fierce voice,
"Who are you looking for, and where do you come from?"

He was obviously very angry and white froth formed
at the sides of his mouth.

"I'm sorry I've entered your home," stammered Ochola.
"But I happened to be passing here and I..."

"There's nothing to be sorry about," the old man
answered, cutting him short. "You're another Luo, aren't
you? And you've come to settle like the rest of them? But
who put it into your head that this is no man's land, for all

Luo people to come and settle as they please. You come like masters to rob us of our land. You want us to work for you, but you don't want your children to work for us. You appoint yourselves chiefs and oppress those who have no quarrel with you. Why do you think I didn't come to your homestead? Did you not find me here? Why should you come before me in this manner? You can rule your own people, they're here by the hundreds, but keep out of my way. You may go now, Chief, and don't come back here again."

By this time Ochola had gathered courage. His belly felt warm as though some juice was boiling inside him. His underarms were wet with perspiration and small beads of sweat covered his nose.

"Is this how you treat strangers who come to pay their respects? Why should you hate me so much? You've never seen me before."

"Leave me alone," the old man jeered at him. "I don't have to know you. Guinea-fowl will not bring forth a chicken, but a guinea-fowl. The rest of you Luo are big-headed, boasting bastards who cheat themselves that they were born to rule. I'm warning you. Be quiet if you want to stay here, and don't approach me as master to a servant. I am my own master. Take yourself back to your own home and be master there!"

The old man walked back to his hut, but instead of entering, he stood at the threshold, resting his hand on the pillar that supported the roof. He eyed Ochola walking numbly towards the gate. Luo people were no friends to nurse at one's doorstep. They seemed all right outwardly, yet they were so uncompromising and stubborn in their behaviour. You are a friend to a Luo so long as you accept his ideas, but the minute you want to think independently there the friendship ends. The people had given in to them long enough, and he, an old man, would not budge an inch, not like the Zangazi tribesmen who had been almost absorbed by the Luo. Their women had refused to marry the Zangazi men because they were circumcized, so the Zangazi had stopped their circumcision ceremonies. When they married Luo girls, the women insisted that the children must learn their mother's language. Thus the whole clan degenerated and eventually appointed someone from Nyanza to rule over them. Stupid Zangazi! Their surname made him feel sick! He spat on the ground!

By this time Ochola had wriggled through the narrow gate. The old man spat again on the grass before entering his hut. Underneath he knew that these people were cunning and that they usually won in the end. But he must put up a good fight! They must know that others were men like themselves.

The path was winding and rough, but Ochola walked on. The dark clouds, gathering in the sky, became black. Ochola was shaken; he felt those strong, red eyes peering at him. His home came in sight and he wanted to run, but his legs felt as weak as a helpless man caught in a nightmare, unable to move.

Nyapol was not at home. The girl who helped her sat nursing the baby on the mat near the granary. The hens pecked about, finding food for their young ones; the village was pleasant and peaceful. Ochola pulled out a stool and sat outside his hut. Presently he saw Nyapol coming to the gate, balancing a water-pot on her head. He did not like the manner in which the old stranger had spoken to him. Such a man was capable of doing much harm, particularly when his village was so near. He did not like those snakes either, and the way they had entwined round the old man's feet. His home must be protected from the old man's evil eye. He would search for a medicine-man to find some plants to dig in round his house.

Nyapol walked past Ochola and put the water-pot down. She murmured a word of greeting and Ochola replied coldly. He wanted to tell Nyapol the whole story but something inside him made him keep quiet. Women were often panicky. Nyapol might jump to the conclusion that danger was just round the corner and make a big issue out of it. He would tell her about protecting their compound but this was quite a normal thing, particularly when you were not sure who was in the neighbourhood.

The cows started wandering in from the pastures. Ochola abandoned his unpleasant thoughts and attended to them. There was no need to fear the old man unnecessarily. He would keep out of his way from now on.

When the work was finished and Ochola joined his wife in the house, he said casually, "I was thinking that perhaps we should find a charm to protect our house. We live amongst strangers and one never knows if there are enemies around."

"That's a good idea," Nyapol agreed. "Now that you've decided, don't leave it too long. Tanganyika is a strange country and we shouldn't take any risks."

They had supper and went to bed. Ochola was relieved that he had been able to make the suggestion of having a charm without his wife questioning him. He would not tell her about his visit to the old man. He wanted to avoid complications.

That year Ochola had the biggest harvest he had ever known. Some of the maize cobs were so huge that a child could not eat a whole one by himself. The millet was fat and the beans were plentiful. Ochola built three granaries for maize and two for the millet and beans. The seeds were stored in drums in the house.

Nyapol was pleased. She had been married for less than two years, yet she had more food stored than her mother had during her twenty years of marriage. It was a pity they were so far away from their relatives. She wanted to share her abundance of food with her relatives, particularly with those who were old and could not cultivate their own land well. Nyapol offered prayers to her ancestors, taking new seeds in a calabash and sprinkling them towards the setting sun. She felt certain that her mother-in-law, whom she had never seen, had blessed them with much food, so it was right to share the harvest with her. Nyapol hoped that, in return, the spirit of her mother-in-law would bless her with more children.

When the harvest had all been brought home, Ochola spoke to his wife.

"Daughter of the Lake, you have not brewed any beer for me since we have been married. Now we have plenty of millet, take time off to brew a large quantity of beer so that we may rejoice with our friends."

His request alarmed Nyapol. She had never brewed beer since her marriage. Brewing beer was very difficult and if any little thing went wrong the whole preparation collapsed. There were only a few women who could really brew strong beer, and there were many whose hands were unlucky and whose beer would not ferment in time. Nyapol had expected this request for months and now that it had come she felt frightened. She knew the basic rules and taboos that her mother had taught her. A woman must not brew beer at certain times of the month. She must be clean. Nyapol desperately wanted her first attempt to be a success, so she consulted Atiga, who was experienced in these matters. Atiga's instructions seemed simple enough and she also offered to help if necessary.

Nyapol started the process. She put some pure white millet in a large pot and soaked it with cold water. The following day she rinsed all the ashy water from the millet, and put it into straw baskets so that the water could run out. Then she covered it with leaves, and left it for two days. When she removed the leaves, she found that the millet had sprouted and looked like laughing insects. She spread the seeds in the hot sun for three days until they were brown and dry. The grinding took about seven days. It had to be done by hand between two stones, a little at a time.

Then Nyapol brought large earthern pots and mixed the flour for the fermentation, following the same methods as her mother. Atiga examined the brew in the second week and told Nyapol that she had good hands. Two pots had fermented to the brim, and were quite strong. The third pot was coming on, though more slowly, but there seemed no need to worry.

Ochola kept out of his wife's way during the brewing days. She was trying her hand for the first time and his nosing around would only make her nervous. Nyapol was a good wife! Many people in this new land had remarked how strong she was in the fields and how well she cultivated the land. Her hands were light during weeding time, she had also proven herself fertile in giving birth to a son. If she was able to brew beer, then her qualities as an ideal wife would be complete.

When all three pots of fermented flour were ready, the task of drying the mixture started. Atiga and two other women helped Nyapol with this tedious job. The party had been arranged for the end of the following week. As this was Nyapol's first brewing, she thought it right to prepare a little for Ochola to try before completing all of it. She cooked the dried flour in the evening by mixing the flour in boiling water till it formed a fairly hard consistency. Then she mixed the cold cooked consistency with cold water and left it near the fireplace for the night.

In the morning Nyapol strained the beer into a small earthen pot. When her husband had finished his lunch, she carried the pot and put it down in front of him.

"Try this and see what it tastes like before I set it before the visitors," said Nyapol, anxiously.

Ochola poured some beer into a small calabash and sipped it. He held the fluid in his mouth for a second, swallowed it, then nodded his head. He sipped some more, a second and a third time until he had emptied the calabash.

"Tell me, Daughter of the Lake, are you sure you haven't ever brewed beer before you married me?"

"How could I have done?" Nyapol laughed. "A girl is never allowed to brew beer in her father's home while her mother is still alive."

"Then you are gifted," said Ochola, gratified. "This is the strongest beer I have tasted for a very long time. You and I will go a long way together. My friends will be very impressed."

Ochola relaxed with the beer the whole afternoon and before long another friend joined him and helped him drain the pot.

The party had been arranged for the following Saturday, when most people were at home. It was the biggest party Ochola had ever given, the largest since his marriage day. More than forty couples were invited, most of them friends of Okech who had lived in Tanganyika for many years. By Friday, the shelter for the visitors had been built, chairs had been borrowed from nearby villages and all the food and drink was prepared as far as possible. A bull was to be slaughtered and some chickens killed to give the guests as much variety as possible.

The house was swept clean and Okech lent Ochola two of his workers to help him prepare for the visitors.

That night, as they sat eating their dinner, Ochola felt very important. Within a very short period he had acquired a reasonable amount of wealth, and it was clear that, given time, he would fulfil his dreams of becoming a rich man.

"Has Atiga suggested any names of women who will help you tomorrow?" he asked his wife.

"Oh yes," Nyapol answered gaily. "There are two newly-married women among her friends who are willing to lend a hand. They will be here before the visitors arrive."

"You can certainly rely on that woman," Ochola said thoughtfully.

"Yes! She's a wonderful organiser and she has never once failed us," said Nyapol.

Ochola thought of the numerous times Atiga had willingly helped them, lending a hand here, and giving advice there. It was through her efforts that Nyapol had settled down quicker than he had expected in the new land. Ochola kept awake far into the night thinking how he was going to entertain and impress the guests who were coming to his home for the first time. If only he could make a name for himself, be thought important, amongst them.

The long awaited day arrived. The sun was bright and the sky was clear. Atiga and the two young women came soon after breakfast, filled with happiness and good will. The two women were introduced to the family, and after having some tea, they set off to work. They fetched water, cleaned the cooking pots and eating utensils, prepared the food to be cooked and checked the general appearance of the shelter.

101

At ten o'clock, the visitors started to arrive. They came in twos and fours, and by about eleven o'clock the village was full of happy, laughing and talking voices. Ten of the most important visitors were shown the bull which was to be slaughtered. Drinks were served while the cooking continued, under the supervision of Nyapol and Atiga. The most important guest was Okech, the son of Sipul, who had been Ochola's right-hand man since his arrival in Tanganyika.

Women in their colourful dresses sat at one table, and talked about their families. Messages which had been received from the motherland were shared amongst them, so that they felt they were keeping in touch with their relatives across the lake. Since they had no radios or newspapers, these gatherings were a useful way of exchanging information.

The men discussed trade and new methods of farming. Occasionally they talked about some of their neighbours who were not of their people, and who did not see things in the same way as they did.

The food was served at about two o'clock. There were large quantities of meat and stew and also some roast or fried meat. There was rice, potatoes and several dishes of fish for women, who in those days were still not allowed to touch chicken or sheep, or drink tea with milk. At a small table in one corner of the shelter was a pot of tender raw meat with *ojuri* which was always given to the older people at these parties. There was so much food that, although the visitors came back for second and third helpings, there was still plenty left by the end of the meal. Nyapol caught Ochola smiling at her as they were clearing away the dishes. A warmth rushed through her. She knew that her husband had been impressed by the quality and quantity of food she had prepared.

When everything had been cleared away and the tables re-arranged, the traditional harpist and his followers came into the shelter. They were going to sing and entertain the visitors for the rest of the evening. The harpist was well known and had won the hearts of his people by singing famous songs, relating to the deaths of important men and women in their society. He sang of Dulo Omolo, the son of Owiti, who had died on his wedding night, leaving his bride alone in her hut. The women cried and the men bowed their heads, in memory of the man whose name they knew so well. He sang of the marriage of Semo, the daughter of Okelo. When he spoke of Semo's beauty and the wealth of her people, the women stared at him with glittering eyes. His voice reminded them of their own young days when they were brides, listening to the praises showered on them by their in-laws.

Now and again, members of the audience interrupted the harpist, and stood up to say their *pak* ("praise") names. This very old tradition provided an outlet for entertainment whenever a harpist played. Okech, the son of Sipul, stood up and addressed the harpist.

"Is that you, the harpist?"

"This is me," the harpist replied proudly.

"Do you know me?" Okech asked the harpist.

Keeping both his hands in his pocket, he puffed out his chest and turned this way and that to show off to the audience.

"How can I not I know you, the son of Sipul," the harpist smiled, pulling a string on his harp as a sign of appreciation.

"Then listen to my *pak* name," Okech said boastfully.
"I am the carrier of a bicycle."

He looked around for his words to sink into his listeners.

"I am the carrier of a bicycle. I am a back of a bicycle
where you carry ugly, shy girls who don't know how to
keep a conversation going with the gentlemen."

The men roared with laughter, looking at the women,
while the women giggled, in agreement with the son of
Sipul.

"Have you heard my name?" Okech asked the harpist
who had now stopped laughing and was listening
attentively.

"I have," he answered, amidst the tunes from his harp.

Okech took out a twenty shilling note from his pocket
and placed it in front of the harpist saying, "Now there
is no more playing unless another member of the audience
puts forty shillings in front of you."

He sat down and two women got up and boasted,
"We stand here to wipe out the footmarks of Okech, the
carrier of a bicycle, who has just stood before you."

They dropped some coins in a plate before him. There
was a murmuring amongst the men before another man got
up to release the harpist to play.

Ochola had never seen this man before. He was tall,
and very well-dressed. He looked younger than most of the
guests and it was obvious that he had been to school. He
cleared his throat and looked boastfully at the audience.
Then he turned to the harpist, who looked at him attentively.

"Listen to me," he said. "I am a female mosquito, a
female mosquito which lands on the skin first before biting."

The harpist and audience roared with laughter. For a few seconds no one could hear what the female mosquito was saying.

A voice called, "Yes, you are right, these female things are so cunning, you know them."

The laughter got out of control as all male eyes turned to the women.

The man quieted the audience and pulled sixty shillings from his pocket.

He put this before the harpist saying, "I dare the harpist to play for at least one hour without interrupting so that we can hear the women's names."

The harpist, no doubt pleased with himself, played two very sweet songs, one in praise of Okech, the carrier of a bicycle and the other one in praise of Ogalo Yambo, the female mosquito.

As soon as these two songs were finished, a very beautiful slender woman got up. The women looked at her with some degree of jealousy, while the men beamed with happiness as if her standing before them had disturbed some hidden emotions. She could not have been more than eighteen years old. Her skin was the colour of coffee-beans and her curly hair was tied with a silk headcloth, leaving some parts showing near her ears. Her cotton dress fitted to perfection and reached only to the top of her knees. Her legs and arms were well formed but dainty. Her teeth were even. The neat small traditional partition in the upper teeth completed her beauty. Her smile was bewitching and when she opened her mouth to speak, the audience held their breath.

"Do you know my name?" she asked the harpist shyly.

"No," the harpist said encouragingly. "Say it, beautiful one. We are eager to hear it."

She looked at the audience once more and then spoke in a low clear voice, which was sweeter than that of a nightingale.

"I am Atai, the daughter of Odera-Nanga. I am a mechanic who has made herself new and beautiful teeth which are too good to be used for eating vegetables."

She gave a broad smile and her dimples were as deep as pigeon-holes. The shouts of the audience encouraged her.

"Would you like to hear my other name?" she asked.

"Yes, yes," the audience shouted and the harpist sounded two very sweet chords in praise of her charm.

"I am Atai castor-oil, the oil that is given to cause diarrhoea to girls who lack a slim waist-line!"

She stood there proudly like some girl at a fashion show, while the men laughed and cheered hysterically. The women without slim waist-lines sat smiling uneasily. She dropped several shillings for the harpist before proudly resuming her seat.

The harpist sang in memory of beautiful women who, during the tribal wars, had made the men fight fearlessly to defend their land. As the drinking continued, more men and women got up and announced their 'praise names' and told of their wealth and the things that made life full and interesting for them.

Nyapol, who had now been released from the kitchen work, and was sitting among the women, once more felt the joy and warmth of a people she loved. She had thought that coming to Tanganyika would move her away from her people whose traditions were part of her life, but there was no need to worry. As long as such gatherings were held ever so often, she would retain the strong ties that held her close to her own people.

At sunset, the party came to an end. Several speeches were made, praising the hand that had brewed the strong sweet beer. They praised Ochola for his hard work, his friendliness and for the generosity which he had shown to his countrymen. They were convinced that in a few years' time Ochola would be one of the richest men in the land. As each guest left for his home, they blessed their generous host.

Ochola stood at the gate to watch the last of the visitors leave. He pulled down the shutter on the gate and walked towards the shelter to help his wife clear up for the night. He was tired and slightly dizzy, as he had drunk more than usual. Nevertheless his happiness for the success of the day was immeasurable. Nyapol had played her part well and the house-warming party must have boosted their status among their friends. They were invited to many parties during the following months.

One day, not long after their party, Nyapol woke up with a headache and felt sick and dizzy when she got out of bed. She prepared breakfast moodily, trying to forget her physical discomfort which had taken her by surprise. Her baby was only nine months old and was still suckling. She did not realise that she could conceive a second child so soon. She left her husband having his breakfast and hurried to the river to draw water before it grew too hot. She walked slowly and thoughtfully, feeling aware of the life that was starting in her womb. As she was busy filling her water-pot she saw another woman hurrying towards her empty handed. Her first thought was to ignore her, as she was not in the mood for talking, but the woman walked straight up to her and greeted her.

"Good morning, my neighbour," said the stranger.

"Good morning," Nyapol answered, coldly, leaving her water pot half filled.

"I have been meaning to come and talk to you for a long time, but as my husband won't let me visit you, I haven't had a chance. That is our home," she said and pointed towards the isolated little village on the crest of the hill.

Nyapol now remembered that when they had moved to their new house Ochola had told her about an old man who lived in that isolated village and who was jealous and hostile towards the Luo people.

The woman continued, "I hope your husband was not very upset by the way my husband spoke to him when he came to our home some months ago. I have been longing for a chance to apologise to him."

"When was that?" Nyapol asked her in surprise.

"Well, I cannot remember exactly but it was some time back. I'm sure he came in good faith but my husband refused to welcome him. It was all very embarrassing."

"I see," Nyapol said slowly. "My husband never told me about this visit."

She paused.

"Why didn't your husband welcome him?" she asked curiously.

"Well, you see," Aziza said casually, "my old man is a medicine-man and he does not like people intruding into his privacy. We hardly have any friends at all."

A cold chill ran through Nyapol's spine, making her scared and helpless before the thin woman standing before her. She thought of filling her water-pot and leaving the woman standing there, but words seemed to force themselves out of her mouth.

"What kind of medicine-man is your husband?" she asked without thinking.

Ochola had not mentioned his encounter with this family but here was her chance to find out for herself.

"I have never been able to discover exactly what he does," Aziza said sadly. "I cannot tell a lie and say I'm happy. It's been a nightmare ever since I married him, having to live in a home which is haunted by evil spirits and snakes. Marriage is a chancy business! Sometimes I wish I were a girl again. I'd never marry!"

"How can you speak to me like that!" exclaimed Nyapol in horror. "I'm only a stranger. Why don't you run away and return to your own people if you feel like that?"

Nyapol felt very frightened. Perhaps Aziza was trying to tell her something more serious.

"I know it is wrong to talk to you like this," Aziza said tearfully. "But you are not a stranger. Being a woman like myself, you can understand. I have often thought of running away and returning to my people, but I know that his hands will never leave me. That's why I decided I must stay with him."

Aziza looked from side to side as if she thought she was being watched, but there was nobody around. She turned to Nyapol appealingly and said, "Promise you'll talk to me whenever we meet. I draw water a little way away from here and I can always walk over to talk to you if you don't mind."

"You are welcome," Nyapol answered politely, hiding her thoughts.

Something told her that the woman had been sent to spy on her. They parted and Nyapol walked home to find Ochola busy milking the cows.

She was upset by the encounter with the strange woman, and the fact that Ochola had never told her about his visit to the old man's home made her angry and resentful.

As soon as the milking finished, Nyapol went up to Ochola and asked flatly, "Why did you never tell me that you visited the old man's home when we first moved here?"

She looked past him so that he could not see the large tears that gathered at the corners of her eyes.

The question came as a great shock to Ochola. He had in fact pushed the nasty episode out of his mind.

"How did you come to know about this?" he asked quickly.

"Why didn't you want me to know?" she said, refusing to answer his question.

"See here, Daughter of the Lake," Ochola's voice became soft. "There's no need to begin the day by quarrelling about something that happened several months back. It was in your own interests that I kept quiet about it. I thought it it would upset you."

"Well, it's upsetting to hear about it in this way," she snapped. "You should have told me so that I knew what kind of people they are."

Then Nyapol bubbled out all that Aziza had told her that morning when they had met at the river. Ochola then told her about his visit.

"It was brief," he said. "There was nothing particularly unusual about it, except that the old man refused to offer me food and was most unfriendly. I was made to feel unwelcome. I didn't stay long. That's all there is to it. I would advise you to forget what this woman has told you, lest her husband feels that we are spying on him. We have our own home and there's no need to fear the old man and his medicines. Our home is blessed and protected and you can rest assured that nothing will happen to us."

In spite of his brave talk, an uneasy feeling bothered Ochola when he drove his cattle out to graze that morning. He was annoyed that this woman, Aziza, had found means of talking to his wife. He did not want her burdened with problems. Life had started so well. Nyapol had settled down completely and such talk made her anxious. This might destroy the good work they had started. Ochola himself was not afraid of the old man's medicine but nevertheless, he decided to keep out of his way.

When they had finished supper that night, Nyapol plucked up courage again and faced her husband. Perhaps it was her new pregnancy that made her so tactless.

"Ochola, is it wise for us to stay here after all those things that Aziza told me this morning? I am sure that the

111

old man hates you and might harm you one day. He told you he has harmed many people who have settled here before us. Why don't we leave this place and build a new home across the river where we shall be far away from him?"

Ochola looked at his wife unbelievingly. Surely Nyapol was deliberately trying to annoy him? Yet he knew Nyapol would not joke with him about such important matters as a home.

"Do you mean to tell me that we should leave this lovely house and rich land and go beyond the river to start life again right from scratch? Look at this big house we have built. Look at the amount of work we have put in to make this compound what it is now. No, I shall not move across the river, or anywhere else. I have no quarrel with the old man. I have no grudge against him. If he wants to harm me without cause, let him try. But I shall live here and die here. If each time an unfriendly neighbour opens his mouth, we have to move to a different place, we'll never have a permanent home."

Nyapol sulked at her husband's uncompromising attitude, but she did not try to continue the discussion.

From that time on, Ochola knew that his wife was starting to imbibe evil thoughts and fears. These were going to be difficult to uproot unless he found some way of dealing with this Aziza.

6

The new seeds had not been planted when Nyapol gave birth. She had twins. They called the first one Opiyo, meaning "the first born of the twins," and the second Adongo, "a daughter born last." The cleansing ceremony usual after the birth of twins was not performed. Some of their friends were Moslems, and others were Christians who no longer believed in such rites. Their homeland was so far away that none of the women there would have dreamt of making the long and tedious journey for the ceremony, even had the news of the birth reached them in time.

The omission of this ceremony added to Nyapol's fear of the fiendish-hearted old man. She became convinced that if she was not cleansed properly, the babies might die. She began complaining about little things, often adding that it was a terrible thing to live so far from one's own people. Sometimes she wept bitterly. It so preyed on her mind that she had not carried out the traditional custom that eventually Ochola sent an urgent letter to his younger brother, Abiero, asking him to bring some of Nyapol's in-laws to Musoma, to carry out the required ceremonies and free Nyapol from her bonds.

When Ochola told Nyapol of these arrangements, she relaxed and forgot the worries of the past few months. Seeing people from home would make life different for her. They would free her from her bonds and make her family safe.

Ochola's easy success in business and his generosity amongst the people living around, had increased the old man's hatred for him. If Ochola kept on throwing large parties month after month, people would start saying that he, the old man, was unfriendly and mean. But since Ochola kept out of his way he found it difficult to pick an open quarrel with him.

In the middle of the weeding season, Abiero and four women arrived in response to Ochola's letter. They were the first visitors from home since Ochola and Nyapol had left their motherland nearly two years before. They were given a rousing welome and were treated with much affection throughout their stay.

In the evening, when the women were talking amongst themselves, Ochola asked Abiero about his father.

"How has he taken my absence?" he asked sadly.

"He is getting over it. You've been good, writing so regularly. He thinks you're different from those who never keep in touch with their families once they leave their home land. But you must visit him soon, he is too old to live long."

They talked about many things concerning their homes and the friends whom Ochola had left behind. Abiero was impressed by the hard work and the wealth that his brother had accumulated within a short time. When Ochola asked him if he would come to join him in a few years' time he readily agreed.

"Of course, it's important to care about home ties, to want to live and to die in the land of your forefathers, but as the world is changing so much, wealth and comfort is becoming more and more desirable."

On the morning of the third day of the visit, a private cleansing ceremony was arranged. Special songs were sung and dances performed. At last Nyapol was free of her bonds and her children were assured of a long and prosperous life. In the evening, Ochola's friends joined the family for food and drink. When the party was over and the visitors had left, Abiero and the women were convinced beyond doubt that Ochola had been right to move to Tanganyika. The women admired Nyapol's clothes and were quite envious of her. They told her that she was very lucky to live in such luxury when most women of her age group were only living in small huts. Nyapol acknowledged the remarks of her sisters-in-law with humility.

"All credit is due to God who has rewarded Ochola for his hard work," she said shyly.

The women wanted to stay longer, as a relaxation from their home chores and to see more of the country, until

Abiero reminded them of their husbands and the children they had left behind. They left after a week but promised to come again and bring their children.

Ochola gave Abiero many things and money to share with his father and step-mother. Ochola told him to assure his father that as soon as the children were old enough to travel they would visit him. The women were very pleased with the generosity shown to them by Ochola and his wife. Each of them received a new dress and beautiful head scarves; also bundles of sugar, salt, and soap. As Nyapol waved them good-bye at the pier, she shouted cheerfully, "Safe journey." They waved back happily. When they arrived back home, they told every one about Ochola's wealth and generosity. His home, they said, was as big as the D.C.'s house at Kisumu.

The old man sighed with relief when Abiero told him that Ochola intended to visit him in a few months' time. He listened attentively as Abiero gave him a detailed account of Ochola's wealth, the big harvest and the number of cattle and chickens he owned. He sent silent prayers to God, thanking him that his beloved son had prospered, and began counting the weeks, hoping each day that a letter would come with the news that Ochola was on his way.

After the cleansing ceremony and the visit of her relatives Nyapol had blossomed like a flower. She forgot the worries and the anxieties that had gathered in her heart, and threw herself wholeheartedly into her work. She had a target to work towards: to help Ochola clear the fields and have everything stored away before starting off on their long-awaited visit to their own people. She imagined how happy her mother and sisters were going to be to see her. She calculated how much money she would need to buy new clothes and head-scarves. The thought of taking three children to see her mother made her so happy that she often kept herself awake at night, thinking about it.

One evening Ochola was resting near the granary. He had been trading cattle at a nearby market, with some success. He heard the squawk of a dying chicken outside the hedge. He snatched up a club quickly and, beckoning his dog, Nyilaji, he scrambled through the small opening at the back of the house. Nyilaji dashed in front of him with his nose to the ground. Presently Ochola heard the wild cry of a cat. He ran towards Nyilaji and when he reached the scene, found the dog holding a large black cat in its paws. The cat had been bitten so badly on its neck that it died soon after Ochola arrived.

Nyilaji stood aside while Ochola examined the cat carefully. It had two small white spots on its chest. Assuming that it was wild, Ochola dug a hole in the garden and buried it. Leaving it lying outside to rot would bring flies and a bad smell into the house. He was annoyed that he had not killed the cat with his own hands. It must have been the one that had eaten so many of his chickens and eggs. Anyway the cat was dead now and that was that.

Ochola told Nyapol, at dinner time, that he had at last killed the wild cat which had been such a menace to their chickens: neither of them gave the incident another thought.

The following day was wet and showery and Ochola was forced to return home earlier than usual. He let the cattle graze within the compound. There was plenty of work to be done at home. Several granaries needed to be repaired for a start. But Ochola felt too tired to start this, so he just sat on the verandah of his house smoking his pipe.

119

"It's funny," said Ochola to his wife, who was peeling potatoes outside the kitchen. "When we were poor, we hardly had enough work to do, and now we're getting rich we have more work than we can manage. I used to think that rich people had nothing to do but sit around and enjoy their money."

"Those who have servants can do that," Nyapol cut in.

"But we have quite enough help, my dear," said Ochola truthfully. "You like doing your own housework, and I'm sure you wouldn't stand interference from anyone even for a day. I thought that relieving you from the heavy field-work would leave you with plenty of time on your hands."

They were still talking when they heard yelling and shouting. It came from the direction of the old man's compound. It was a woman's voice. Nyapol knew that Aziza was often beaten but this was the first time that they had heard such a terrified cry. The yelling and shouting died down just as suddenly as it had come. Aziza never cried for long, simply because there was nobody who could go to her rescue. The sound of raised voices was carried by the wind towards Nyapol and Ochola. The old man was talking at the top of his voice.

"Where is my medicine-cat? Where is my medicine-cat? Answer me quickly," he said threateningly to his wife.

"I don't know, I don't know," his wife sobbed loudly. "How can I tie up an animal with four legs? It wanders where it likes."

"You are here to look after my things," the old man thundered. "How often have I tried to knock this into your head, and you still won't listen to me."

120

Aziza's cries died down. As the wind started blowing in the opposite direction Ochola and his wife did not hear any more of what was said. They soon dismissed the scene as a normal row between husband and wife. It had nothing to do with them. Ochola got up and started milking the cows.

The old man took his club and left his homestead to look for the cat. It was he who had trained the cat to steal Ochola's chickens, so he knew where to look first. He followed the narrow path near the river till he reached Ochola's enclosure. A mound of earth, like a little grave, brought him to a standstill. He noticed some blood stains on the grass nearby and hairs that looked like a cat's. His heart started to beat furiously. He quickly dug up the earth with his stick. He slowly pulled out his black medicine-cat — dead and stiff!

The old man wept as he wrapped the dead cat in a goat's skin. Thoughts raced round in his head. Should he burst into Ochola's home and challenge him to an open fight? No! He decided against that. He knew the answer Ochola would give him and he was not going to let him get away with it. He took out a piece of bamboo from his pocket and emptied the contents of the hollow stem into the pit. He covered it carelessly and then walked back slowly to his home. After sunset, he returned to Ochola's village. It was dark and nobody could see him. Ochola was playing with the children and Nyapol was busy cooking the dinner. When the old man started to plant medicine all round the fence, neither Ochola nor his wife heard him.

The family sat down to supper.

"I like your cooking," Ochola remarked. "You cook just like my mother used to, when she was alive."

Ochola never praised anything without mentioning his mother's name and Nyapol was used to it. They talked for some time, and as he was in a good mood, Nyapol took advantage of it.

"I have now had three children, but my mother has never seen any of them," she said. "The months seem to be passing away and we don't seem to be hurrying up with our plans to visit our home as we promised Abiero. I don't want to give mother the impression that I'm lost. Let's fix a date to go and see them," she begged.

"Well, I'm glad you've reminded me," answered Ochola. "It's high time we fixed a definite date. Then we'll write a letter to let our people know in good time. When we get to Seme, we can arrange the number of days that you can spend with your mother."

They talked for some time about who they would ask to look after their home, of the things they would take with them, and how many days they would be away. Nyapol had scored her point and she was very happy about it. She put the children to bed, then she joined her husband at the table and they talked well into the night. Before they slept, Ochola told his wife that he felt a little feverish.

"You never believe in medicine, that's what's wrong with you," his wife said slowly. "How many times have I told you to take medicine when you're sick and you won't listen to me?"

"Don't give it any thought, Daughter of the Lake. It's not as bad as you make out. I have a weakness for telling you little things that should be overlooked."

Then they both slept, but at about two o'clock in the morning, Ochola woke up. He thought he heard someone

122

walking about outside. The dog barked once. Overpowered
by sleep, Ochola closed his eyes, and forgot about the
footsteps and the dog's barking. Then he had a dream. He
was sitting on a rock by the riverside, watching his cattle
drinking. As he sat there, he saw the old man walking
towards him. He was carrying some maize meal in his left
hand, and as he approached Ochola, he broke off bits of the
meal and threw them on the ground. It looked as if he was
throwing food to the chickens. He was shouting, and the echo
of his voice rang loudly through the thick forest. His bitter
words reached Ochola's ears but instead of getting up and
fighting, he just sat there motionless, as if he were rooted
to the spot.

> "You Luo people, you Luo people,
> What kind of people are you?
> I hate all of you.
> You cheat yourselves that you were born to rule
>   others.
> You cheat yourselves that you are the only good
>   farmers,
> That you know how to make money and keep cattle.
> You let your land fall into the hands of the white
>   men.
> The white men will steal away all your land from
>   you.
> You work little, but you eat much.
> For you every day is a party!
> Return to your land all of you!
> If you don't, give me back my cat alive
> If not, you will pay for it!"

Still dreaming, Ochola saw the old man's figure disappear
into the river below. The cattle were gone and he was sitting

alone on the rock. He tried to move, but could not. His body did not seem like his own and his hair had changed into long white thorns, which made him look like a porcupine! Ochola woke out of his sleep, paralysed with fear, his body covered in perspiration. He threw off the blankets and tried to sit up. But he felt sick and giddy. His ears buzzed and stars passed in front of his eyes; he thought he was going to faint.

He fought the peculiar feeling and sat upright. It was too clear to be a mere dream — he shouted and his voice woke Nyapol out of a deep sleep.

"Whatever's the matter?" she asked quickly, putting her arms round him, and trying to quiet him. But Ochola continued to shiver, and muttered some words as if in his sleep. Nyapol jumped out of bed and looked for the lamp. She opened the cupboard and hunted for the bottle of quinine which she kept there. She poured a spoonful and forced it into Ochola's mouth.

Ochola swallowed the medicine in one gulp.

Immediately he started shouting, "Old man, old man why are you killing me? Why are you after my life? I killed your cat because I thought it was a wild one. I killed it because it was killing my chickens. You wronged me in the first place, didn't you? Deny it! Deny it!"

Nyapol was terrified. The long buried fear of the old man's medicine rose up afresh. She sobbed loudly.

"Ochola, Ochola, I told you to leave this place. I pleaded with you to move beyond the river and go away from this wicked man, but you wouldn't listen to me. You mustn't die. Oh, son of Kisero, don't die."

But Ochola jumped out of bed and almost knocked his wife to the ground, as if Nyapol's words had turned him out of his mind. He flung the door open and rushed outside. Hesitating at the gate for a few seconds as though he was listening to something, he then ran off into the night. Nyapol tore after her husband. It was already dawn and very cold. The mist covered the entire surface of the earth making it difficult to see ahead. After chasing Ochola for about half a mile, she lost track of him. Then she remembered she had left the door wide open and the children alone in the house. For a moment she stood still, her heart torn in two. If she followed her husband, something might harm the children; yet if she returned to the children, she would be unable to help the man she loved. She looked round. She was alone. Her teeth chattered from fear and cold. She decided to go back to the children. They were still sleeping peacefully when she entered the house. She sat on the edge of the bed and wept bitterly. There was nobody she could turn to, except Okech. But Okech's home was some miles away and, as the area was infested with wild animals, she feared to leave the children alone in the house. However, something told her to go to Okech's house and break the news to him immediately. She looked at the children again — they were fast asleep with their little ayah by their side.

Nyapol picked up her coat and wrapped it round herself. She blew out the lamp and went outside and locked the door. She started running. The fear of wild animals and poisonous snakes vanished from her mind in her anxiety for Ochola. When she reached Okech's village the sun's rays were just peeping through the morning mist. The gate was half open and Okech was in the yard, milking. His wife was busy sweeping when Nyapol burst into the house. She ran towards her with open arms, noticing her tear-stained face.

The family gathered round Nyapol to hear her story. Atiga stood with her hands folded across her chest, the children quietly holding her skirt. Okech saw that Nyapol found it difficult to find words to describe what had happened.

"Daughter of the Lake," he said kindly. "What news have you?"

Nyapol pulled herself together and told Okech's family about Ochola's dream and how he had run away from the house.

"He was panting like a mad man," she said, recalling the horror of those few moments. "Then he disappeared into the forest. I tried to follow him, but the children were alone in the house, so I had to go back to them."

Nyapol raised her voice and sobbed aloud.

"Son of Sipul, I know you have done so much for us since our arrival in this land," she continued, "but don't turn your eyes away from me at this hour or I'll be doomed. Do you know a medicine-man who could free Ochola from this terrible curse before it's too late? I've no one else now. My life and the lives of my children are in your hands."

Nyapol could say no more. All the emotional strains and hidden fears of many months had come into the open. She now had no doubt that to leave one's motherland to go and live as a stranger amongst strange people was a sin in the eyes of the ancestors. Okech's family were shocked to hear the news. Atiga wept while Okech sat waiting for Nyapol to calm down.

When her sobs had become quieter, Okech said anxiously, "I didn't know Ochola had any enemies. Who could this evil-eyed man be who is out to destroy the son of Kisero? The son of Kisero's heart is as clean as a child's. Can you remember anyone who has been unfriendly towards him?"

When Nyapol spoke again, her voice was clearer. She told Okech how jealous the old man had been of Ochola, ever since they had built their home. She told Okech of Ochola's visit to his home many months ago and what he had seen, and how the old man had threatened him. Then she told him how Ochola had killed the cat that had been eating their chickens, and how it turned out to be the old man's medicine-cat.

"Why didn't Ochola tell me any of these terrible things?" Okech asked gravely. "I'd warned him that Tanganyika was a strange land, full of jealous men with eyes to destroy their successful neighbours. I could have protected him from the start if I had known, but now he has given the enemy an advantage over him."

Okech got up and left the two women sitting alone in the yard. When he came back he said there was not a moment to lose, as Ochola's life must be in danger. After a few words with Atiga, he decided that a message must be sent to Ochola's brother, telling him what had happened. Then he would look for a medicine-man.

Okech called his son and said, "Son, prepare yourself for a journey. You must leave here tomorrow to go to Seme to find Ochola's brother, Abiero. Tell him he should come at once, for Ochola is sick and Nyapol and her children desperately need his help. Don't waste time on the journey and bring Abiero back with you. Do you understand?"

"Yes, father," the son replied.

He liked Ochola and was willing to do anything for him in this time of need.

When all this had been decided, Nyapol walked home. Okech promised to call and tell her as soon as there was any news of the medicine-man.

"Have mercy on me, have mercy on me! Father, the Father of the children of Ramogi, and the Comforter of the friendless, have mercy on me!" Nyapol found herself praying alone as she walked.

The sound of yelling, frightened children greeted her as she turned in at the gate. She ran to open the door.

They rushed towards her, crying in a chorus. "Where have you been? Where is father?"

"Father is sick," she replied.

"But where is he?" they demanded. "Have you taken him to hospital?"

"No," said Nyapol gravely. "He's not gone to hospital. He's run away and disappeared in the bush. When we've eaten, I'm going to look for him."

"In the bush? Where?" the older child asked, in disbelief.

"When you've eaten, I'll tell you more," she said.

The children did not understand what their mother was saying but they were so hungry that, for the moment, the food made them forget about their father.

Ochola found himself in a part of the forest where he had never been before. He felt feverish and the blood drummed in his ears. His eyes were swollen and painful from the glare of the bright sunlight. His body was sore. The hairs on his skin stood up in thorn-like warts, pricking his body till he became listless with pain. He could not sit down or lie on his side. When the wind blew hard, he felt as if his whole flesh was being torn away from him. He moved carefully, avoiding any bush that might touch him. He was naked, apart from a loose sheet which was tied round his neck and hung over his body. Above him, the birds sang, while all around him the monkeys jumped from tree to tree. There must have been fierce, wild animals in the vicinity too, waiting for darkness to fall to go hunting, though Ochola did not think of them. He was not even conscious of his surroundings, or that he was a husband, a father, and a wise man. All the things that had been so precious to him had gone out of his head. He only thought of the grave where his tortured body could lie in peace.

In the afternoon Okech called on Nyapol, as he had promised. Atiga and a few women friends were there with her. The medicine-man had been summoned, but Ochola was nowhere to be found. They all decided to go out into the forest to look for him. But the day's search ended without their finding any trace of the missing man. They went again on the second day and then the third. They combed the bush from dawn to dusk, but each evening they came home without him.

On the fourth morning, rumours were heard that some human bones had been found by the riverside. It was said that a man had been mauled by wild animals. Many people started saying that it must have been Ochola. The news shattered the minds of the searchers, and the wives tried to stop their husbands from going out into the forest.

"What's the use?" they asked. "Ochola is dead. He was devoured by animals and you might be next!"

So the number of searchers decreased daily, but Nyapol refused to believe that her husband was dead. She told Okech repeatedly that she felt sure he was alive but had lost his senses and could not find his way.

Nine days had passed since Ochola had disappeared and there was still no news of Oloo, the young man who had been sent to fetch Ochola's brother. Atiga became worried about her son, and could not hide this from her husband. Okech remembered having told his son firmly not to delay but to return at once with Abiero.

"It ought to have taken him four or five days at the most," he said. "But now, nine days have gone by, and we have had no news of him. Something must have happened to him."

Okech found himself worrying about his son night after night. He had lost Ochola, his closest friend, and now his son had disappeared.

The children asked their mother daily, "Where is Oloo? Where is Oloo?"

Their numerous enquiries saddened the parents, who could only answer "We don't know."

Meanwhile, Oloo, with many other passengers, had been marooned in the steamer, s.s. "Busoga", which was to have carried them from Musoma to Kisumu. When they reached Port Bell, they were not allowed to dock for several days. There was an outbreak of small-pox and no one was permitted to travel from Uganda to Kenya until he had been vaccinated.

They were held up at Port Bell for nearly a week because the Medical Officer said that he must see the results of the vaccination before they could disembark. Oloo urged the captain again and again to let him go on by road because he was on a very important mission, but the captain would not listen to him.

Meanwhile the African "bush telephone" had conveyed the bad news ahead of Oloo.

Abiero was standing on a cow-shed in the market on Monday morning, when a man ran up to him and asked, "Is it true that your brother Ochola has gone mad and run away from home and disappeared into the forest? Please don't hide the truth from me."

Abiero looked at the man gravely. "Tell me how you heard such news?"

"Everybody is talking about it, all over the country," the man told him. "They say he went mad and ran away from home and disappeared into the forest."

Abiero left the man without further questioning. He untied his goats from the shade of a tree and walked towards the main road, avoiding people who might ask questions.

Rumours heard in the market places were rarely true, but Abiero could not ignore this piece of news. He was most upset that such dreadful news could have reached other ears without his family knowing anything about it. He took the shortest possible road and walked on, hardly looking where he was going. He did not know how he would break the news to his father. The old man was very weak and he might be shocked beyond recovery.

131

At sunset, the family assembled in the old man's hut to arrange for Abiero to go to Tanganyika. His father took the news calmly, but he went without food and spent the day smoking his pipe and sipping small amounts of home-made beer to soothe his nerves. Relatives had arrived. Some were weeping while others were smoking and drinking or just standing around talking in low voices. The old man reminded the family to stand together, so that if suffering and sorrow came to them, they could meet it with strength in unity.

Abiero would leave at dawn to make the journey to Tanganyika. He must find out if the rumour he had heard in the market was true. While they were still making preparations, a young stranger walked in. It was Oloo! Though the news had indeed reached Seme before him, it was not his fault.

The boy was given some food and when he had eaten, the family sat in silence listening to his message. Oloo obeyed his father's instructions to say as little as possible, lest the old man should have a heart attack. The messenger had been on his way for nearly two weeks, and no one knew whether Ochola was now alive or dead.

The family decided that Abiero should accompany the young man the next day. They should return to Tanganyika on the ten o'clock steamer. But when the young man told them that there was an epidemic of smallpox in Kisumu, and that the pier was closed, they decided to take the early morning bus to Busia. From there they could travel by road to Port Bell where they could catch the first boat to Musoma.

Neither Abiero nor the young man had travelled through Uganda by road before, but luck was with them, and they arrived at Luzira late in the evening. They found a small boat ready to sail to Musoma. Abiero ate little and did not sleep that night. He wondered what news awaited him. His father had told him to bring Ochola home if he found him alive.

The next afternoon they hurried to Ochola's home with sinking hearts. The evening was nearly gone when Abiero and Oloo arrived. The cows were restless, bellowing to be milked. Nyapol was dishing out supper for the children when she caught sight of Abiero at the gate. She put down the food and ran to meet him. She had made up her mind not to cry but as she reached up her hands to greet him, she broke down and wept bitterly.

"Why have you taken so long?" she sobbed. "I've suffered so much alone in this strange land. It's almost three weeks since we sent Oloo to you. What happened? Tell me quickly."

Abiero ignored Nyapol's questions and asked her anxiously if she had heard any news of Ochola.

"There's no news," Nyapol told him gravely. "The men called off the search, saying that Ochola must be dead in the forest. But I don't believe them. I keep on praying and hoping that one day he'll come home, but as the month closes in, my faith is weakening."

Abiero's heart sank. All the way he had kept on thinking that he might find Ochola at home and that he would nurse him back to health. He walked past his sister-in-law into the house, looked round the sitting-room. It was empty except for the crying children. He went into the bedroom and the bed was empty. He went into the visitors' room, but that was

133

empty too. Then he came out and stood in the yard with his hands above his head, the way women do when someone has died.

He wept bitterly, saying, "My brother, my brave one. How can you die before I have seen your face once more? It is you who carry the burden of the family! You are our hope. How can you die before blessing us!"

Nyapol's feelings were roused afresh and she wept again. Ochola's children were gradually accepting the fact that their father might never come back. They would be like Juma, whose father had died when he was a little boy, so young that he could not even remember him.

Oloo went to tell his parents that he had arrived safely, after a hazardous journey. After supper had been served, Nyapol told Abiero how the trouble had started between Ochola and the old man and how things had worsened when Ochola killed the cat, mistaking it for a wild one. She told him how Ochola had run away from the house and how everyone had combed the forest day after day, but in vain.

"Now everyone thinks that my husband is dead but I keep on thinking he's still alive. But how can he live in the forest for three weeks without food? Perhaps the people are right and Ochola has joined our mother in heaven."

Abiero said nothing. The children were sleeping, and Nyapol and her brother-in-law sat by the fire in silence. There was so much to think about that the little lamp had burnt out by the time they went to bed. The next day would be the beginning of the fourth week since Ochola's disappearance.

That night, Abiero had the same dream that he had had on his way to Tanganyika. His dead mother was telling him not to return to Seme until he had found Ochola. When he awoke he felt his mother's presence in the room. He could sleep no more. The dream had scared him but it gave him hope. He would, indeed, search for his brother. If he was alive he would find him and bring him home.

When Okech and his wife arrived at Nyapol's house the following morning, they found Abiero about to go into the forest to start looking for his brother. They had breakfast together, while Okech told Abiero where they had already searched. Abiero thanked him for the help he had given the family by sending his son to fetch him. Okech said he would go with Abiero and spend two more days in the forest. But they found no sign whether Ochola was dead or alive.

Okech said it was useless searching the forest any longer. But Nyapol and Abiero refused to believe that Ochola was dead and Abiero said he would go on looking for his brother.

The cold spell started unexpectedly, and although Abiero suffered greatly from the heavy rain, nothing would keep him at home. Every evening he returned late, very depressed, and often refused to eat. He began to lose weight.

One evening, when Abiero was returning home, he stopped for a while to rest his weary feet. He sat down on a flat rock, facing the golden rays of the setting sun. He took some boiled maize cobs out of his bag and started to eat. His mind wandered back home. He thought of his wife and children, and remembered his father's last words, "If your brother is still alive, bring him home."

And he remembered the voice of his dead mother, also urging him to find Ochola. Tears burned in his eyes. He did not know when he would be able to go back to his family. The forest was full of wild animals and highly poisonous snakes. Would he ever survive? He decided to pray. He lifted his eyes towards the sky and faced the sinking sun.

"Bless me in my trouble, God of Ramogi," he said aloud.

The big red ball disappeared behind the mountains and darkness began to fall. Suddenly he heard a voice calling, "Abiero, Abiero."

He looked round but he saw nobody. The voice kept calling, "Abiero, Abiero."

Fear gripped him. Someone was, indeed, calling him, but he did not recognise the voice. Was it a ghost or a human being?

"Abiero, Abiero."

Could it be Ochola?

He called out, "Ochola, Ochola, where are you? I've searched for you, I've mourned for you. Come, show yourself if you're here!"

Ochola slowly emerged from a cave under the very rock on which Abiero had been sitting.

The brothers stared at each other. Ochola looked like a ghost! Abiero was tempted to run for his life but his feet were rooted to the ground. Seeing he was afraid, Ochola spoke.

"Abiero, don't run away from me! I'm your brother, Ochola."

But Abiero was still paralysed with fear. The man standing in front of him was half naked; his face and limbs were like that of a human being but his flesh was completely covered in thorn-like warts. He looked like a human porcupine.

"Ochola, is it you, my brother?" asked Abiero weakly.

"It is," was the faint reply.

When Abiero ran to embrace him and to tell how they had all been searching for him, Ochola raised his hands to stop him.

"Don't touch me. I'm mad with pain; these thorns on my body tear my flesh to pieces. I have wandered in the forest looking for the road which would lead me home, but I have not been able to find it."

Abiero plucked up courage and forced a smile.

"Ochola, I've found you! At last I've found you! My heart will rest now. Come home with me now before it gets dark."

Abiero took his brother's hand and led him through the thick forest until they reached the path leading to Ochola's home. They hesitated at the gate. Then Abiero went in ahead to warn Nyapol about Ochola's appearance. Nyapol did not listen to Abiero's words. She rushed past him. When she saw a figure standing there, her heart started to beat loudly and she ran faster. But when she reached the place where Ochola stood, she did not recognize her husband. His appearance shocked her so much that she fell down in a deep faint.

When Nyapol came round she was lying on her bed. Ochola was sitting near the fire, talking to Abiero. Nyapol went towards her husband, and kneeling beside him took his hands and pressed them over her face. She wept until her tears ran down between Ochola's fingers. Ochola's illness had changed him so much that she lost all hope of his recovery. It was a bad omen. What ordinary illness could make a man's body grow thorns? Ochola must be cursed! He was going to die young, before he could enjoy the fruits of his labour. Ochola hid his eyes to avoid Nyapol's grave face. He realised he was mainly to blame for their troubles and he thought it wise to keep quiet. They sat in silence for a long time. Then Nyapol let go of his hands and went to make tea.

Ochola had a burning desire to see his friend Okech immediately, but Abiero persuaded him to wait until morning. Though Ochola's pain was maddening the warmth of the room released him. Supper was brought. He had no desire to eat but took some milk and fruit. That night they sat by him. He could not lie down because his skin was so sore. Nyapol could not sleep. When at last she dozed off, she was haunted by bad dreams. When the children woke and saw their father, they were terrified. They did not seem able to understand that he was their father and refused to go near him. But Nyapol thanked

God that her husband was home at last. She cried and prayed that they would now all return to their motherland.

The news that Ochola had been found spread quickly. Some people said that he had turned into an animal, others that he was a ghost, some even said that he was half-man, half-beast. At first people were frightened to see him but their curiosity was so great that they soon came in great numbers. Okech went to see several medicine-men, and each one claimed that his cures were the best in the land. Knowing that Ochola was very rich, they knew they would earn a lot of money if they could cure him.

The first medicine-man that came and examined Ochola announced that he had treated many people whose condition was far worse. If Ochola followed his instructions carefully, he would be quite well within a few days.

The family looked at the medicine-man hopefully. They believed him, and when he asked for a black bull before starting his treatment, they gave him one. The medicine-man then washed Ochola's body with some herbs and gave him some liquid to drink. He left him some ointment to rub on his body twice a day. That night Ochola did not sleep at all. The pain was worse than ever. His flesh burned and his fever returned; at times he was nearly unconscious. On the third day, Ochola was worse. The family decided that they must call in another medicine-man, but Okech decided that it was better to ask the same one to return. They sent for him but he was nowhere to be found. On the fourth day he came and saw that his patient was indeed dying. He changed his medicine, still assuring

141

the family that Ochola would survive. On the sixth day he returned again, but when he saw Ochola, he threw his hands in the air.

"My friends," he cried. "This spell is stronger than my medicine. I have done my best, but I've failed. Forgive me and let me go in peace."

Abiero and Nyapol thought of the bull they had given away for nothing. Several more medicine-men came, all claiming to be able to cure Ochola's disease. But soon after they had taken their payment they too announced that the disease was more powerful than their medicine.

Ochola grew thinner and weaker each day and Abiero and Nyapol began to lose hope. Both of them knew Ochola could not live much longer.

* * *

The sounds of the drums filled the air and the people were dancing well into the night. It was the time of the annual harvest festival but in Ochola's home there were no joyful preparations. The minds of the family were centred on the emaciated, sick man. Nyapol had urged Abiero to take Ochola back to his home so that he could be buried amongst his people. But because of the strange nature and severity of his illness, they could not use any form of public transport.

Nyapol was feeding the twins on the verandah, when her eldest son, Safari, came running to her, shouting, "Mama, mama, a visitor is coming!"

Abiero who was bending over Ochola, turned round to look. Sure enough, there was a stranger at the gate.

Abiero went to meet him and they shook hands and exchanged greetings. Abiero invited him into the house.

Nyapol greeted the visitor coldly. When the formal introduction was over, the stranger told them that his name was Magungu, the son of Owuor, from Kanyada in South Nyanza. He said he had heard of Ochola's illness and would like to be given a chance to cure him.

Nyapol listened to what the visitor had to say, then she replied, "Yes, like the rest of them you've come to get easy money, to take away the few things we have left. What will the mourners eat when Ochola is dead? Many medicine-men have come, speaking hopefully just as you're doing now, but after they've taken their fat gifts, they try out their cures and then say, 'Your husband's disease is too powerful for our medicine, you had better look for someone else.' Every man who comes thinks that his medicine is the best in Tanganyika. I suppose you want to take your share like the rest of them?"

Magungu was silent under the torrent of words.

Then he said quietly, "Would you like me to try, or shall I go? I can't treat your husband unless you believe in me."

Nyapol was not really interested. Magungu looked even less intelligent than the others, and they had failed miserably.

"All right," she said suddenly. "Go ahead if you like, but I don't think you'll be any different from the others."

Abiero encouraged Magungu to stay and try his treatment. He said that Nyapol had been so unhappy that she had little hope left.

143

While Magungu and Abiero were having tea, Nyapol went into another part of the hut to feed the babies. From where she sat, she could just see her visitor. Magungu was unkempt, his matted hair was so shaggy that he looked like some madman. His long twisted beard joined with the hair from his head, and his shabby moustache looked like a cat's whiskers. But that was not all. His eyes were as red as those of a cattle egret and one of his front teeth hung so loosely that it moved up and down while he spoke, as if it would fall out at any moment. A strip of goatskin was tied round his wrists, and a large cow's bone hung down his chest.

Abiero took Magungu outside to the *siala* tree, where Ochola was resting. Magungu introduced himself and told Ochola that he would like to try his medicine on him. Ochola said nothing. He stared at Magungu as if he were the angel of death.

Ochola beckoned to Abiero and whispered, "Ask him what payment he requires, we have so little left."

Magungu heard him. Turning to Ochola he said, smiling, "How can I ask for payment before treating a patient? How do I know I'll be able to cure you? If luck is on my side and I do succeed, then you can pay me. But if I fail, I shall take nothing from you."

The two brothers looked at one another in surprise. All the other medicine-men who had visited them would not even examine Ochola without first being paid.

Abiero went to milk the cows, while Nyapol busied herself preparing the evening meal. Magungu sat near his patient and looked at him. He asked many questions which put Ochola at ease. When, at last, he suggested he should start the treatment, Ochola felt he could trust him. He called Abiero and Nyapol into the house. Magungu fetched his medicine-bag. Inside were calabashes, bamboos, bottles, animal skulls, and cowrie shells of different sizes and colours. After bathing his patient he made several scratches all over his skin, and then rubbed in medicine from the different containers. Abiero and Nyapol watched his work.

The first and second nights passed and the sick man still lay groaning on his bed. Nyapol sat by her husband's side nearly all the time. Sometimes she wished she could share his suffering. She would rather suffer actual physical pain than experience the ghastly nightmares that came to her during her fitful sleep. Sometimes she felt senseless with sorrow and pain like a woman who has given birth to a still-born baby. If God was there, why did he not help her? On the third day Ochola improved a little and that night he slept soundly. When he awoke, the sun's rays had filled the room. He turned his head round slowly. For the first time for many weeks, his mind was clear. What did puzzle him was the noise. The birds were singing louder than he had ever heard them before, and the sound of the hungry calves, the pecking chickens and the playing children made his compound sound like a market place.

Magungu appeared in the doorway and Ochola turned his head and asked, "What's all this noise about? It sounds like a market place this morning."

Magungu grinned.

"There's nothing unusual, Ochola, nor is it your imagination. You've been too ill to hear all these noises. Try to ignore them, you'll soon get used to them again."

At about nine o'clock Nyapol came in with a bowl of porridge. When she saw her husband, her heart leapt with joy. Ochola greeted her with a faint smile, and a hopeful expression, which she had not seen on his face for a long time. She wanted to run out and tell the children that their father was better, but she knew it was too soon to be happy. She must control herself in case the evil spirits might again change her happiness into grief. Ochola finished his porridge and handed the empty bowl to his wife. She lingered near him in case he wanted to talk to her. She longed to hear his voice. When Magungu entered the room, Nyapol took the bowl and left. She went into her dark bedroom and wept. She could not stop sobbing. All the emotions of the last few weeks bubbled up inside her. After a time she pulled herself together and started preparing the midday meal. Her heart felt lighter, and she found herself thinking of happier days gone by: the monthly parties they had held to entertain their friends, the new dresses Ochola had bought her without her asking, and how many women envied her marriage with a rich man like Ochola who was contented with only one wife.

Would they still envy her now? Were they sympathetic to her? Did they plead with God to turn her grief into joy? Perhaps they were not even thinking of her and those who were thinking were probably just saying that she had had it too easy.

God was teaching her the hardships of life.

She added salt generously to the vegetables and started cutting up the meat that was to be prepared for the patient. Maybe he would drink some soup if she could put a little effort into preparing it.

146

Abiero, like his sister-in-law, kept calm about Ochola's improvement. Magungu had said that he must not be asked continually about Ochola's progress. He would keep them informed about his condition. Except for Okech, he refused to allow visitors to enter Ochola's hut.

Some days later Magungu told Abiero that someone was coming near his home every night. On several occasions he had heard footsteps. Now that the patient was getting better they should guard against any setbacks. They must keep watch, but as it would be difficult to do this without Ochola's knowledge, they decided to tell him. Abiero and Magungu kept watch in turns, for several nights, but they saw and heard nothing. Then, on the fourth night, after a heavy thunder-storm, Magungu heard footsteps near the hedge, close to the patient's hut.

Magungu touched Abiero's hand in the darkness. Yes, he had heard the footsteps too! They discussed in whispers what to do. At first they thought of releasing the dog to chase the intruder, but Magungu decided against it. It was only a few hours before dawn and the rain had nearly stopped. Magungu would plant heart-shaped beans in the footmarks and fill them with medicine. When the beans became swollen, the wicked man's feet would swell. Ochola slept on and his dog did not bark.

At dawn Magungu went out to look at the foot-prints. He made some stilts, two long poles with steps for feet, so that he could propel himself along without his feet touching the ground. He left Abiero and Nyalaji, the faithful dog, waiting at the gate. Magungu searched a wide area. He searched until the sun rose in the sky but he

147

could not find any footmarks. He walked round the whole compound, but found nothing. Later on, they set Nyalaji free. The dog ran round the homestead several times and came back disappointed; it could not trace the scent.

Nyapol joined the two men under the *siala* tree, where they were eating their porridge. Magungu told Abiero that he was more disturbed than before. He was already finding it difficult to deal with the old man's medicine, and now, if the sounds they had heard last night were those of ghosts, the situation would be still more complicated. Looking at his gloomy face, Abiero felt drained of all courage. Nyapol asked Magungu whether it would be possible to take Ochola back to Seme. Would it not be wise to move Ochola to his birth-place before any more harm occurred? She stood looking away from them, her eyes resting on the edge of the world where the earth kissed the sky.

Magungu was picking his teeth. He did not look Nyapol in the face, but spoke as if talking to himself.

"If it was my will, I would take the son of Kisero home to-morrow. The first son of his father should die in his own home. He would like it that way. He has often told me so. But luck is against us. The only thing we can do is to purify the house and hope that his skin will return to its normal condition."

The family accepted Magungu's advice. Nyapol now trusted him implicitly and humbly asked him to forgive her for the unfriendly words she had spoken on his arrival. She felt that as long as he stayed with them, they were safe from harm.

Magungu wanted a white cock first thing in the morning, so that he could start work before sunrise. This presented a problem! There was only one white cock left and Nyapol had refused to part with it. When the medicine-man from Ukerewe had demanded a white cock for sacrifice, Nyapol would not let him have it, but her faith in Magungu made things easier for him, and when Abiero told her that Magungu needed the cock, she reluctantly agreed to let him have it.

At sunrise the following day Magungu started his work. He decked himself out with green creepers which he had pulled from shrubs near the river bank at dawn. He looked terrifying. He took medicine from the bamboo containers and sniffed it up both nostrils. Then he took his medicine-spear in his hand and a strange power came over him. He darted across the compound with his nose in the air, like a man possessed with a strange spirit. The children shrieked and yelled because Magungu looked like a strange animal wanting to devour them. Nyapol kept them in the house because she was scared of the outcome of the purification.

Magungu took the white cock in his hand, and talked to it like a fellow human being.

"Find the red pot for me, it's here in the village, find it now," he said.

Then he chopped off the cock's head with a sharp knife. The headless cock ran round until it fell into the old fire-place. Magungu rolled aside the cooking stones and furiously dug up the fire-place. The dead cock lay beside him. Nyapol watched, holding the baby tightly to steady

149

her hands. She felt sick with apprehension. Suddenly
Magungu pulled up a red pot and stared at it. Abiero
moved nearer, trembling. Nyapol walked out into the yard.

"Help Ochola to come and sit near me, he must see
these things with his own eyes," said Magungu, over his
shoulder.

Abiero obeyed, and he and Nyapol stood near the
patient but the scared children kept out of sight. Magungu
lifted out the contents of the pot with his medicine-spear
so that the family could see them. First he pulled out a stiff
dead snake, then a tortoise, a rat and lastly, a monkey's
arm. Nyapol fainted.

Magungu rubbed some ash on her forehead and she
regained consciousness. She turned her head and caught
Ochola's eyes. His rugged face looked lifeless, as if all
the blood had drained out of it. Were they thinking of the
same thing? What they had witnessed was a clear sign
that Ochola would never get well unless Magungu possessed
super-human powers.

Magungu dumped the pot and its contents in the middle
of the compound. He roasted the chicken hurriedly, like
someone who had not eaten for many days. When it was
ready he started to cut it up. Something attracted his
attention! The cock had the largest crop he had ever seen.
He pulled out the muscles holding it, and cut it open. He
looked at its contents curiously. Nyapol clung to Abiero's
clothes and looked away as Magungu walked towards them
with the contents of the crop. There were bird's claws, small
sharp thorns that looked exactly like Ochola's warts, bits

of hair and many other small objects. How on earth could the cock have swallowed all this sorcerer's junk?

Magungu broke up an old basket and, throwing the pieces over the miscellaneous collection, he set fire to it. Abiero and Ochola were talking in low voices. Ochola's spirits sank after seeing the things that Magungu had found. The gate was locked early at sunset and there was no chance of anyone entering the compound during the day without being seen, but nevertheless, Magungu had found all these things. Nyapol stopped weeping. It was long past their meal-time, but she did not feel like cooking now. The children could manage with some cold food, and later when she had gathered her strength, she would warm up some porridge for Ochola.

The smouldering fire died down and the rough midday wind scattered the ashes leaving only a dark patch where the grass had been burnt.

Magungu joined the grieving family. The children had now come out of the house and were squatting near their mother. Magungu addressed the patient directly.

"Son of Kisero, it is this wicked old man who is killing you. You are a Luo and a stranger here, but you've not remained poor and needy, you've become rich and prosperous in a land that is not yours. Your fame has spread far and wide, while this old man has remained mean and poor in the land of his birth. His shadow has filled this compound. There, look! His shadow is at the entrance!"

The family strained their eyes to see the shadow at the gate, but they could see nothing. Perhaps the old man's shadow was there, in some miraculous way and that was

151

how he had planted medicines in and around Ochola's home. Perhaps he could walk in and out of the compound without being seen.

"Damn the son of Satan," thought Nyapol bitterly.

Their eyes were focussed on Magungu again. He was now their only hope. He had power to see things that they could not. Magungu was silent for a long time, but when he spoke, sorrow and despair struck the whole family.

"My brother," he said, addressing Ochola, "I can't stay any more. I must return to my home. I've worked on you day and night since my arrival, but I'm ashamed to say I'm defeated. This man's power is too strong for my medicine. I ask for nothing from you because I haven't succeeded. Let me return to my home in peace."

He stopped talking and fixed his eyes on the clouds like a man talking to God.

Ochola could not believe his ears. He had not got up from his bed for weeks, until Magungu arrived, but now he was improving daily. He was beginning to enjoy his food and at night he slept. He had hoped one day to be completely cured. Only the previous evening Magungu had said confidently to him, "Give me a white cock and I shall clean up the compound for you! When I've done this, you'll be quite well." And now, after raising his hopes, Magungu was leaving.

Ochola lifted his voice and wept like a woman, saying, "I had no hope when you came to me, son of Owuor. I was a dead man! But you assured me that you could make me whole. Don't leave me, I beg you. Remove these thorns and let me enjoy my life again. Son of Owuor, please don't desert me. You are my only hope. Couldn't you find some medicine that could kill the man who is so bent on destroying me?"

Magungu reprimanded him. "My medicine can't be used to kill. God has given me power to save life, not destroy it. Therefore I can't agree to your request. Let me go back to my home, I pray you. If I can make a stronger medicine, I'll come back. But now I'm defeated!"

Ochola realised that it was fruitless to plead any more with Magungu. He had obviously made up his mind to go. So the great medicine-man collected his things and left for Kanyada, his homeland. He stopped at the gate and looked back for a moment, as though he wanted to change his mind. But he went on. The family watched him until he disappeared along the winding path by river bank.

It was about midday. The lazy wind blew so slowly that nobody was conscious of it. The sun was hot. The weaver birds were making their nests in the eucalyptus trees; their chirping could be heard in the silence.

At the door of the hut, Ochola was sitting on a mat with his back to the wall. He closed his eyes and rested his head. His hopes of going back to Seme, to be buried in his own village, were shattered. He wept. He realized how useless wealth was to him now. Money had no power against such evil.

When he opened his eyes, he found Nyapol standing beside him with his children and his brother Abiero. A little further away from them lay the big family cock — roasted and stiff, lying on top of a coop, with a Luo knife resting beside it. It no longer looked like his old cock, which had been the alarm clock of the whole village for so many months.

8

Ochola's compound resumed the quietness of the months
before Magungu came into their live. Not a peaceful
quietness, a kind of terror: a panic that grips a drowning
man whose salvation is snatched away by a powerful wave.
No one wanted to talk; even the children were quiet and did
not cry. At sunset, when Nyapol took food to her husband,
he avoided her eyes to hide his grief. Her heart ached
for him, as she knelt down besides him and held his
hands close to her breasts. There was nothing she could
say to him and her throat swelled with compassion.
It was terrible to watch him dying slowly, while she was
powerless to help him. Ochola never smiled now and
his rough, haggard face was withdrawn. He looked at
least ten years older than he was. Nyapol dished out a

little food for him, but he refused to touch it. She pleaded and wept, telling him not to despair.

"Food is also medicine," she said. "Just eat a little to keep some strength in your body."

He forced down a few mouthfuls, merely to please his wife.

Nyapol met Abiero at the door when she returned with the dishes. He had finished milking. Instead of going to sit near the doorway waiting for supper, as he usually did, he said he was going for a walk.

"But it's getting dark," said Nyapol, lamely.

"That's all right," he answered in the same tone.

"Don't wait for me to eat, I'm not hungry to-night. If there's any porridge left over, I'll have that when I come in."

Nyapol did not argue. She understood how he felt. All the same she would prepare some food and give it to him when he returned.

The sky was clear and the setting sun looked huge and terrifying. Abiero had never seen it look so fierce, as if its creator was angry with the inhabitants on the earth. He stood, as if fixed to the ground, staring at the flaming ball till it sank behind the earth. Bitterness towards Magungu crept into his mind, but he tried to suppress it. Then he started thinking about his own family. He had been away from his wife and children for two months now. What was his wife thinking? Their second child had just been born when he left her and she had not wanted him to go away. He had assured her that he would soon return. Abiero wondered if he should go back to his family. He would talk it over with Nyapol and see what she said. It was now dark and he turned towards the house. His resentfulness towards Magungu returned. Why had he raised their hopes only to say at the end he was defeated? It was Magungu who had made him write a letter home, saying Ochola was improving and would soon be well enough to travel. Then, just when all their hopes were revived, he had packed his things and left them.

Nyapol had not eaten, but the children had been fed and were now asleep. Abiero told Nyapol about his plan to go home and see if his family were well. He spoke quietly, so Ochola would not hear, but Nyapol urged Abiero to tell him. When Abiero put the plan to the sick man, he would not hear of it.

"Abiero, my brother," he said tearfully. "You know I can't travel with this terrible disease. Wait here until I die, then you can carry my body home and bury it amongst my people."

He turned his face away and refused to talk to them any more.

Ochola's illness became worse. As the days went by, he could not eat or sleep. Once more Nyapol went across to their friend Okech for help. As it happened he had just been coming along to see her with a letter brought by relatives from Seme.

The message, from Ochola's father, said, "If the local medicine fails to cure Ochola, take him to the white man's hospital. Perhaps the white man, with his wisdom, can help him where our people have failed."

The family assembled to decide what they should do. They were sitting in Ochola's room so that he could hear what was in his father's letter.

There were two hospitals within reach. One was quite good, but the white doctor there was not very co-operative. He spoke in his own language, through an interpreter, who often translated the patient's words before the patient had finished speaking.

"Do you think it's worth trying?" Abiero asked.

"We should try everything now," Okech replied. "Abiero, you went to school, you can speak this white man's language. You can tell the white doctor all that has happened."

Nyapol kept quiet throughout the discussions. She had seen so many different kinds of medicine tried on her husband, that she did not think that the white man's medicine would do him any harm, even if it did not cure him. She hated the smell of hospital wards, but for his sake, she would put up with it.

When Ochola was asked if he agreed, he said there was nothing else to do. It was the only hope. He had seen all the medicine-men for miles around. Magungu was brave and wise; yet he had gone, saying that the illness was too strong for his medicine. Only the white man's hospital was left.

In the afternoon Okech returned with a van belonging to Abdala Khassim, a Nubian trader from whom they bought food. Abdala knew Ochola and agreed to take him to the hospital, thirty miles away, at a reasonable price. Ochola was wrapped up in a clean white sheet, since he could not wear any clothes. They laid him on a sisal mattress at the back of the van. Okech and Abiero went with him, leaving Nyapol to look after the children.

"Is father going back into the bush?" Safari asked tearfully.

"No, father is going to the white man's hospital," Nyapol replied.

But her answer made no sense to the child. He had never seen the white man or his hospital.

Nyapol pressed Ochola's hands.

"Be brave, my husband! My heart goes with you."

She turned away.

Then the van moved off and Nyapol and her children stood at the gate weeping, until it had disappeared in the distance.

The party arrived at the hospital at three o'clock in the afternoon. Abdala who had taken many sick people to Pembe Tatu Hospital, was familiar with the routine. He drove straight to the"Out-Patient" department and parked the van. There was a long queue of sick people. Abdala walked past them to the office and went up to one of the nurses in white uniform. He told her that he had brought a very sick man, who could not walk. The nurse asked the attendants to bring a stretcher and take Ochola to the doctor's surgery.

Dr. Thomson peered through his glasses at the patient on the stretcher. He was an elderly man in his mid-fifties, and had worked in several mission hospitals in Tanganyika. Dr. Owen, to whom Okech had referred earlier, was the young man who spoke no other language but English. He was on holiday at the moment, and Dr. Thomson had been called in to take on his work. He spoke Kiswahili almost as fluently as he spoke English, and knew several other local languages besides. He was an Evangelist as well as a doctor and used to preach the Gospel of Christ when he had any spare time. He glanced at Ochola and decided that he must be admitted straight away to the Isolation Ward, where he would be thoroughly examined. Okech and Abiero helped the two male nurses carry the stretcher along to a four bed-roomed ward, which was kept specially for patients with contagious diseases. They lowered Ochola on to a bed, and prepared him for the examination. The two male nurses fled in horror as soon as they saw Ochola's body. They disappeared, leaving Okech and Abiero alone with the patient. They feared to look back in case they should catch the terrible disease.

The word quickly went round amongst the nurses that a "half-man-half-animal" had been admitted to the Isolation Ward. Such a man could haunt you at night, so they did not want to go near him. When Doctor Thomson came to examine the patient, there was not a nurse to be seen. He called for them and at last found one hiding in the sluice, pretending to be cleaning bed-pans. Doctor Thomson understood their feelings. Ochola did look fearful, but he was very annoyed that the nurses had deserted their patient.

He went over to Ochola and frowned when he saw his body.

"How did this illness come about?" he asked the relatives.

Okech murmured to Abiero that they should stick to one story — and they should not tell the white man too much or he might twist everything round and in the end blame them for refusing to be Christians. One man should speak on Ochola's behalf. "You speak to him," Abiero said to Okech.

"Mh," Okech cleared his throat. "Well, the sickness came on him suddenly one day when he came back from herding the cattle. That night he had a fever and didn't eat. Towards dawn he became delirious. Then he ran away from home into the forest. When we found him, his body was covered with these things."

Okech looked up, relieved. The first question had been answered well. Now he waited for the second. Dr. Thomson finished writing and looked at Okech again.

"How long has he been sick?" he asked.

"For two weeks," replied Abiero.

Okech was more nervous now because this was actually the third month of Ochola's illness. But it would spoil their case to say that they had kept him at home all that time.

"Only two weeks?" Dr. Thomson said sarcastically. "He looks as if he has been sick for a whole year."

Okech kept quiet.

"How have you treated him during these two weeks?" Dr. Thomson asked, not looking at Okech's eyes.

He hoped to gain these people's confidence, then perhaps they would tell him the truth.

"Well," said Okech, clearing his throat again. "We were using our own medicine."

"What makes you bring him here now? Why didn't you bring him last week?" asked Dr. Thomson.

Okech hated speaking to these white men, their talk was full of 'why, why, why.'

"We hadn't saved enough money, Doctor, to pay for the transport or to pay hospital fees," replied Okech quickly.

Okech stood waiting for a reaction from Dr. Thomson about his carefully thought out lie. Dr. Thomson went on writing without comment. Then he put down his notes and stood up. He faced Okech squarely.

"You were trying your native medicine on him. You've failed and you've now come to us as a last resort. Do you expect me to perform a miracle and restore a dying man to life?"

Okech did not reply. This white man with his pair of glasses, and a set of teeth as white as chopped cassava roots, might possess the power to read thoughts. It was wise not to argue with him.

Realising he could get no more information from the relatives, Dr. Thomson asked them to wait outside. He then examined Ochola carefully. In his twenty two years in Africa, he had never seen a disease like this. He had never seen a human body grow thorn-like warts. He looked closely at the emaciated, disfigured body lying curled up on the bed. What could be the matter with him? The patient had no temperature, his stomach was not distended. There was no rigidity in his neck or loss of power in any part

of his body. There was nothing to suggest that he had any
malignant disease of the brain. Yet looking at him, he
seemed half dead already. The expression on the faces of
his relatives showed clearly that they had given up hope.
Dr. Thomson put a needle through one of the jelly-like
warts, thinking they were full of fluid, but nothing came out.
He then scraped off a piece of skin and sent it to be
examined under microscope. But when all the examinations
and tests were over, nothing helpful was revealed and Dr.
Thomson told the anxious relatives that he could only keep
Ochola in hospital under observation. He told them he had
never seen such a disease before, but that he would use all
modern methods to restore Ochola to health.

So Okech and Abiero said "Good-bye" to their brother
and returned home to wait and pray as the white man had
told them. Darkness was falling when they arrived and told
Nyapol the results of their journey. She listened tearfully
and a flicker of hope stirred in her heart when she was told
the white man's words.

That night Dr. Thomson waded through all his medical
journals and books on tropical diseases. He tried to find
something that might throw light on Ochola's terrible
illness. He found nothing. In the morning he spent several
hours with Ochola looking at his body and re-examining him.
But when he had finished he was none the wiser. His work
was made even harder when the nurses declared that they
were scared of Ochola and refused to nurse him. One of
the male nurses who had helped when Ochola was admitted,
went down with an attack of violent ague and a severe
headache. He talked in his sleep, shouting out that the new
patient was strangling him. Even Nurse Elizabeth, who was

a strong pillar of Christianity amongst the hospital staff, refused to go near Ochola.

Dr. Thomson was stranded with a hopelessly sick man. Anger mounted in his heart. Did the nurses expect him to look after this man by himself? Didn't they realise that he was a doctor and had other work to do? He gave Ochola two injections and walked slowly to his house to tell his wife that there was a crisis at the hospital.

"I think you are too lenient with the staff," his wife told him, when they were having coffee. "These nurses are paid to do their work. If they don't do it, don't pay them. It's simple."

Dr. Thomson looked at his wife sadly.

"It's not as simple as you think," he answered. "Africans are not like our people. They have no sense of vocation, like you and I have. We are serving our Master, Jesus Christ. They have no Master to serve. Not many parents want their children to work in hospitals as nurses, because it is a dirty job. We can't be really tough with them or they'll simply leave and go home. How many times have nurses in this country thrown their uniforms at us and returned home? It would be foolish to risk a walk-out here, when I have only come as a relief doctor."

"What do you intend to do with the man then?" Mrs. Thomson asked stubbornly.

She drained her coffee and put the cup back on the saucer with a bang. Dr. Thomson hesitated a little and then faced her.

"Well," he said, "I was just going to ask you to lend us a hand while Sister Moore is down with fever. As soon as she's up, she'll take over."

Dr. Thomson clutched his coffee cup tightly. He did not even know why he had decided to tell his wife about the patient with the strange disease, let alone ask her to help nurse him. He had not thought of doing so when he walked away from the hospital. Now he waited nervously for her answer.

She looked at him for a long time without speaking.

At last she said, "I think you're mad, Roy, completely mad. What have Africans done for you? You go on giving and giving to these people and they'll never be grateful for what you do for them. If they're afraid to die from this man's disease, what about me? Surely Roy, you must be fair. If both of us catch this disease and die, who'll care for our children? And will the black people remember that the Thomsons died nursing their people? Never!" She spat out the last word in disgust.

"If I believed in witchcraft, Roy," she said slowly, "I would say that the Africans have bewitched you. Have you forgotten what the strikers at Knopper's Sisal farm shouted? 'Only a dead European is a friend.' Remember, Roy, remember?" Mrs. Thomson turned bright red all over her face.

She got up to go before saying any more, but her husband gripped her arm tightly.

"My dear," he said gently. "What bitter words to come out of a heart where Christ lives. Isn't Christ big enough to protect us from all these diseases? Anabel, have you forgotten what Christ has done for us? It's only a suggestion, anyway, my dear. If you don't feel like helping I would not persuade you. After all, whatever you and I do for these poor people, we do it for the Lord. And if we die while in God's service, our reward will be great in Heaven."

Dr. Thomson left his coffee half finished, and walked back to the hospital. He was not angry with his wife. He knew he had asked too much of her. What really bothered him was that Anabel's quick temper might one day stop her entering the Kingdom of God. He would hate to be there without her!

Ochola was groaning with pain when Dr. Thomson entered the ward. He was swollen all over and his eyes were so puffy that he could not even open them. He was breathing with difficulty and his jelly like warts had doubled their size. Dr. Thomson acted quickly. He ran to the "Dangerous Drugs" cupboard and prepared an injection. He plunged the needle into Ochola's arm. Then he sat by his side and felt his pulse. After a while it returned to normal and the patient's breathing became easier. He sighed with relief.

Mrs. Thomson called Hussein, their house servant, to clear away the coffee cups. She started helping to prepare lunch. Hussein did not talk to her, and she felt embarrassed. She knew that Hussein had heard her and her husband quarrelling. Hussein was a Moslem and Mrs. Thomson was already trying to convert him to Christianity. Maybe now Hussein was despising her. Moslem women were humble creatures, their husbands were their masters. They worshipped them, and lowered their veils each time they saw another man coming in sight. Hussein had told her one day, that there was nothing bad about women covering their faces when they saw the men outside the family. It was a sign of respect to their own men folk.

Mrs. Thomson left sure that Hussein was looking down on Christianity, because Christian women like herself shouted at their husbands and looked them in the eye. She left the kitchen and walked out into the garden, pretending to be collecting flowers. She did not want to behave the way she did, but her husband's madness about his patients often irritated her. Not only that, Roy's Christianity was sometimes taken too far. He was always turning the other cheek to the Africans and as a result they had no respect for him. If Dr. Owen had been there, no nurse would have refused to touch that patient. If any had refused, they would not have remained in the hospital compound for another day. He would tell them to go before they had the cheek to walk out. That was how to set an example to the other nurses! Mrs. Thomson reached the bottom of the garden and stood there staring at a big tree. The red flowers looked just like the flame-tree picture which she had seen in a book. She stared at the tree without moving and the fear that God was looking at her, made her afraid. Could it be that God was speaking to her the way He spoke to Moses in a burning bush? The tree with its flame-like flowers looked like a burning bush. Mrs. Thomson lowered her eyes lest God was there and she feared to look at Him. The feeling was so vivid that she felt God had truly spoken to her. She hurried back to the house trembling and went straight to her bedroom to pray and to ask God's forgiveness. When Dr. Thomson returned from the hospital at lunch time he found his wife waiting, tearfully, to tell him that God had spoken to her in the garden. She was now truly sorry for what she had said.

167

"Roy, I will nurse that patient," she cried.

Dr. Thomson listened to his wife attentively. Tears glittered in his eyes. He believed every word she had told him.

"I always tell you that God appears to us at the time of need, my dear," he said, and hugged her close.

It was heart-warming to know that they were both once more walking on the narrow road that led to the City of God.

At two o'clock Anabel Thomson walked over to the hospital. She went straight to the Isolation Ward, to the patient whom the nurses had refused to care for. She was shocked when her husband uncovered Ochola's body. She had never seen such a strange disease. She was terrified and almost begged her husband to let her go back. Then she remembered that God was with her on this enterprise.

Ochola lay resting and Dr. Thomson explained to him that the African nurses had refused to stay with him. Mrs. Thomson, he said, who was a trained nurse, had agreed to help. Ochola gave Mrs. Thomson a long searching look, and turning to Dr. Thomson he said quietly, "She will help me."

From that day on either Dr. or Mrs. Thomson stayed with Ochola day and night. They tried many medicines on him. Dr. Thomson made a special trip to Musoma township to get one of the drugs that he had read about in a medical Journal but, whatever treatment he received, Ochola reacted badly. He either developed a rash or his body became swollen.

Nyapol went to hospital on the second day, and listened while the doctor explained to Okech and Abiero that Ochola was not responding to any of the medicines they had tried so far, but that he still hoped to find a cure. Ochola was drowsy from the sleeping-pills that he had been given but was not feeling so much pain. As they walked home, Nyapol was more worried than ever. She still feared that her husband would not come home alive. Nyapol could not find anyone to stay with the children, so after this visit she stayed at home while the men went to see Ochola as often as possible.

At the end of the week Ochola's condition remained unchanged. Dr. Thomson prayed earnestly that God would reveal some new treatment. He would collect money from the brethren to pay the bill if Ochola could not afford the money. He would save him at all costs. That night Dr. Thomson wrote a long article to the British Medical Journal. He enclosed several pictures of Ochola to support his description. He also wrote a separate letter to his friend Dr. Marsden, a skin specialist at a London hospital, asking for his advice on the case.

During the second week Dr. Thomson invited two doctors from Mwanza to look at Ochola. They examined the patient and after going through Dr. Thomson's notes, they said frankly that they had never seen such a disease before. They had nothing further to suggest.

One day Nurse Elizabeth told Dr. Thomson that Ochola's sickness was not an illness that could be treated with European medicine.

"Why don't you let his people take him back so they can try our African medicine?" she asked.

Dr. Thomson looked at Nurse Elizabeth, unbelievingly. "Do you mean, nurse, that African witchcraft is better than our medicine?"

169

He felt hurt and disappointed. He had been practising medicine for over twenty years. Elizabeth had been in the hospital for only two. Now she felt qualified to advise him! What cheek!

"Well, Doctor, this man has been bewitched, or rather cursed, by a medicine-man. It needs another medicine-man, with stronger medicine, to remove the curse from him. Only then will he get better. Western medicine has no power over this type of disease!"

"What makes you so sure that you know about this case, Nurse Elizabeth?" asked Dr. Thomson, softening.

Putting up a resistance would only make the nurse withdraw into her shell. Any suggestion about Ochola's illness might help him in his struggle to cure the disease.

"But everybody in the hospital talks about it, Doctor," said Nurse Elizabeth. "They say that this man is a Luo who migrated here. He became rich in a very short time and became famous. His neighbours resented this, and one of them bewitched him to prove that Tanganyika medicine is stronger than Luo's. The people here are saying that you and your wife are wasting your time trying to cure him. Let him go back to his own people. They may be able to help him."

Dr. Thomson looked at Nurse Elizabeth. He could hardly believe his ears. Pembe Tatu hospital was a centre of the Christian faith; a pillar to several Missions in the land. He had great fellowship together with the staff and he believed that they loved Christ. Yet now he realised that these people were still African, full of 'heathen' practices and 'superstitious' ideas.

170

"They only pay lip service to the Christian God when it suits them," he thought bitterly. "Do you believe these stories, Nurse Elizabeth?" he asked, "You're a Christian, aren't you?" He looked at her gravely.

"We're all Christians, Dr. Thomson," Nurse Elizabeth said, avoiding his eyes. "But as Africans we know that there are bad spirits that cause disease, or a bad eye that causes death. European medicine has no power over these bad spirits. We see so many cases like this. They receive treatment here, but they don't recover. African medicine then cures them."

"Thank you, Nurse Elizabeth," Dr. Thomson said at last.

He had indeed gained some very useful information, but the truth had hurt him. He would not give in and tell Ochola's relatives to take him home. He would go on trying till the relatives themselves asked for the patient's return. Of course there was no such thing as a particular "African" disease that scientific medicine could not cure. But the people themselves were so superstitious, and once they believed they were bewitched, they became resistant to scientific medicine.

Dr. Thomson laboured on. He made fresh tests and tried new drugs. But the relatives were becoming restless and he could tell that they wanted to take Ochola home. Dr. Thomson persuaded them to wait for a letter from England. In the third week a letter came from Dr. Marsden, the skin specialist, saying that he had never heard of such a disease before, in any part of the world! He thanked Dr.

171

Thomson for having sent him the information but regretted that he was unable to help the case.

Dr. Thomson looked at the letter in dismay. Bitter disappointment stabbed his heart, leaving him with a helpless feeling of failure. That night the Thomson family prayed for a long time. They asked for fresh guidance on the way to treat Ochola's illness.

The third week ended. The fourth week began. Okech, Abiero and Nyapol were waiting for Dr. Thomson to arrive.

"My people, take me back so that I can die in my home," Ochola had just said to them. "The white man has nursed me with kindness; he has tried all kinds of medicine on me, but without success. Ask him to give his permission to let me go back home."

At first they argued amongst themselves, saying they should leave him for a few more days. Then they agreed to ask Dr. Thomson to let them take him away. They would not even wait for the letter from England. They were still discussing the matter in low voices, when Dr. Thomson approached. As soon as they had exchanged greetings, Okech put the family's view to him.

"Kind doctor," began Okech. "Our brother wants us to take him home. You've been extremely good to him but since it has not pleased God to cure him, please let us take him home. Don't worry about the letter from England now."

Dr. Thomson started to say that it was a pity to remove Ochola when he was still so seriously ill, but in a way he was relieved. With the disappointing letter from the

specialist there was no hope that he would cure Ochola
even if he kept him there for another month. The only
thing that hurt him was the phrase Okech had used. It had
not pleased God to cure him! Sometimes the Africans had
wrong ideas of God. He did not punish his children in this
way. But Dr. Thomson thought it wise to be quiet. With
such a failure, it was not the right time to preach how
kind God was to a disappointed group of relatives. Perhaps
it was not the fault of these Africans to think differently.
As a Christian, he himself believed in the history of Job and
accepted the fact that God can let Satan sometimes have his
way. Sometimes God has to stand aside to see if someone
really loves Him. This to the non-Christian was an
unacceptable puzzle. How can a person who loves you let
you suffer tribulation and death while he stands aside,
watching? The non-Christians wanted a tangible result. If
God really loves His children surely He should not let them
suffer?

Dr. Thomson turned away from the relatives and went
up to his patient. Ochola made a great effort to thank him
and his wife for the kindness they had shown him. He
would return at a later date if the letter from England
brought good news. The voice of God or his conscience
urged Dr. Thomson to tell Ochola frankly that, in fact, the
letter from England had come, but another voice
contradicted the first one. It would only make Ochola lose
all hope in life to be told that even the wisest white man
in England did not think that his illness was curable. It
was better to say nothing.

"Don't hesitate to return if you wish," Dr. Thomson
told his patient. "I'll give you some sleeping tablets which
should help you to settle down and relieve the pain."

173

Towards mid-day the relatives lifted their sick brother into the same van that had brought him to the hospital. Several able-bodied patients stood outside to catch a glimpse of a man whose illness was stronger than the powerful medicine of the white man. Dr. Thomson and his wife stood looking on with disappointment and pity.

The glaring eyes of the African nurses seemed to say, "We told you that the white man's medicine would not cure African diseases."

9

Nyapol's mood changed completely with Ochola's return from the hospital. Nothing mattered to her any more. All hope had melted away. The desire to return to Seme was stronger than ever. She needed most of all the help of her own people and the feeling of being with them. First she had based her hopes on Magungu, but he was defeated. Then her hopes were raised by the white doctor, but he too had failed. What more were they waiting for, here in Tanganyika? Surely no medicine-men could succeed where the white man had failed!

After washing Ochola and giving him his breakfast, she said, "Ochola, let me return to my people, let me take my children away from this accursed place before some misfortune befalls them. I won't stay here any longer, I've made up my mind to go."

The long-repressed outburst had flared up at last!

Ochola gathered courage and replied, "I know that you're tired of me, Nyapol, and that you don't care what happens to me. But how can you speak of going to Seme with the children and leaving me here alone? It's this kind of talk and threat that harms the life of the children. It's true that the compound is littered with medicine, but none of the children has ever been ill."

"But what is it that makes you stay here, Ochola?" asked Nyapol. "You've a father! You've enough land! Why don't we face reality and return? Perhaps the air of our motherland would cure you. Let's sell everything here. Let's go back home. I'm prepared to nurse you forever, Ochola, if I can only be amongst our people. I'd feel safe there."

"You go home if you like," he said. "But I'll not move. If it doesn't please God to cure me, I'll die here, Nyapol. I won't go. I've told you this before and I haven't changed my mind. You've stood by me all the time ever since I married you, but if you want to desert me now, go. I'm too sick to argue."

He turned his head away from her, dejected and helpless.

Nyapol left Ochola's room — her plump body quivering with anger. Ochola had chosen to misunderstand her all along, and it pained her that he should question her love, when she had spent so many weeks nursing him. In persuading Ochola to return to Seme, she was merely suggesting what was best for the whole family. Ochola comforted himself that he had made the right decision. His remaining possessions would be taken by his enemies. His own people would run away from him and call him a ghost. He would die where he was!

The days dragged on slowly. The nights seemed longer and darker and the ghostly sounds of the crickets and the pond frogs kept Nyapol awake. When day came, she felt listless and exhausted, like a woman in labour waiting patiently for the midwife to tell her that her time has come. Sometimes she sat alone thinking and waiting; waiting for the time to pass away. The maize crop had long passed the weeding stage, and the green leaves were gradually turning yellow. There were huge weeds among the plants, but Nyapol left them to grow. Abiero did most of the heavy work and did not complain. Sometimes Nyapol sang sad songs so that Ochola could hear her. Often she scolded her children for no reason. But Ochola turned a deaf ear to it all.

Then the devil struck again! Nyapol was preparing the grain. Safari, the eldest boy, was playing with the twins out in the yard, when he suddenly fell down, kicking and screaming. Nyapol dashed to him, trembling. As she reached him, he lay absolutely still. Green water like bile was oozing from his mouth. Nyapol shook him frantically. He was not breathing. She grabbed him up in her arms and dashed to the house. She laid him down on the bed and poured cold water over him. The child showed no signs of life.

She shook him, shouting, "Safari, Safari, don't go, don't leave me, don't go."

The child did not answer.

Abiero was out at the time, herding the cattle. Nyapol desperately needed help. Suddenly the child gasped and started breathing again, slowly. Nyapol stopped crying. She prayed, calling the names of her mother-in-law and many ancestors who were close to her heart. Then she suddenly remembered; in her rush to get the dying child into the house, she had forgotten the twins in the yard. She rushed out, and to her horror, one of the twins, Opiyo, lay stiff on the ground. Nyapol dashed to him, picked him up and ran into the house with him and laid him down besides his brother. Opiyo suddenly started to cough, sneeze and cry, all at the same time. She wrapped him up in a blanket and poured a few drops of water into his mouth. The child struggled as if life was departing from him. Ochola crawled on his knees to come when he heard Nyapol's cries. He sat on a mat behind his wife, hands under his chin. He could do nothing to help her.

In despair, Nyapol turned round and said, "All these misfortunes have befallen me because you have refused to return home. How many times have I pleaded with you to let me take the children away from this country, back to the land where they belong? You wouldn't listen, and now it's too late. What have you to say?"

She wept bitterly beside her dying children. Ochola sat in his place, motionless. He knew Nyapol blamed him for everything that had befallen them. Whatever he might say at this time would be wrong.

The children began to improve a little. Ochola moved near and touched them. His wife ignored him but he swallowed the insult, so as to prevent another outburst. Then he crawled back to bed, pleading with God to keep his children safe. That day was perhaps the saddest of Ochola's life. The thought of yielding to his wife's request to return to Seme nagged at him endlessly, but he stood firm on his decision to stay in Tanganyika. Nyapol brought him some soup late in the afternoon. She left it near his bed and did not wait to help him as she usually did. A thought came to Ochola. If only he had two wives, one at least would care for him when the other one was upset! But the thought left him as quickly as it had come. It could be worse when both of them were upset at the same time! That night Abiero sat up with his sister-in-law, keeping an ear open for Ochola's calls.

But misfortunes never come singly. The new day brought another tragedy into Ochola's household. When Abiero went to milk the cows, he found Nyilaji, the faithful dog, stretched full length on the ground near the cattle-pen. It was groaning and its illness looked the same as that which had attacked the children the previous day. The same sort of greenish stuff was oozing from its mouth. When Abiero touched it, it did not move or bark. Abiero felt really frightened. Not only was he afraid to tell Ochola that the dog he loved so much was dying, but now he felt that this disease was so rooted in their homestead that it would kill them all. Why could Ochola not see that their ancestors were not pleased with them? When Abiero told Ochola that his dog was dying, Ochola wept, and refused to believe him. What had he done to the Gods? His children lay in bed seriously ill. He himself was half dead. Now his faithful dog was dying too. All these months, Nyilaji had stayed by his bedside, keeping him company and watching over him. He loved the dog dearly.

179

"Give me a hand, Abiero, let me see my dog before it dies," he said.

Nyilaji was still lying in the same place. Ochola knelt beside the dog and touched him.

"Don't die, Nyilaji, don't die, my faithful dog. I am already half dead. You have to stay here and take care of the family and the home. Please don't die!"

But the dog remained stretched on the ground and did not even whimper. Its eyes were half closed. Ochola knew it was not listening or it would have responded with a lick or a wag of its tail. He asked Abiero to carry the dog to his room. He wanted to keep a close watch on it. But Nyapol would not hear of it.

"You're dying, Ochola. Why can't you rest your weary body, instead of fussing about a dog? Your children were dying here a few days ago, your own children. You didn't once suggest that you wanted to sit up with them or feed them. Now nobody can have a minute's rest in this house just because your dog is sick!"

She spat on the floor, and walked away. Ochola's anger mounted. He wished he was well. Nyilaji had protected them all from wild animals. How could Nyapol forget Nyilaji's bravery and value so soon! Besides, Nyilaji was as good as any member of the family. He was brave, obedient and honest.

In spite of Ochola's fuss and prayers, Nyilaji's condition became worse. One morning the dog was so weak that Abiero and Nyapol suggested to Ochola that they should call the vet, to put Nyilaji to sleep. The dog might be suffering from rabies. But Ochola would not hear of it.

"The vet will have to poison me first before poisoning Nyilaji," he said. "Leave my dog alone!"

He waved Abiero and Nyapol away.

"Let Nyilaji die his own death."

Nyapol left the hut, but she returned after a few minutes and knelt besides Ochola and took his hands.

"Son of my mother-in-law, don't let your sufferings ruin all the happy moments we used to share when you were well. Ochola, you're so ill, and you've gone through so much pain, but we're still man and wife. If God is kind and you get well we may yet have a long life together. Now tell me, Ochola, what's the matter? Whatever I say is wrong. I know you don't want to go home to Seme, sick as you are. I have given in on that. But now this dog. You talk as if everyone except this dog has neglected you since you became ill. You forget the sleepless nights, the immeasurable days, I have sat by you, weeping and praying. Now you insist that the dog must not be put to sleep. Suppose the dog has rabies! Is it fair to have it at home? Suppose it bites one of us, what will you do?"

Ochola thought for a while and then looked at his wife in a new light. Of course he had been touchy and nasty of late, but who wouldn't be, with all the suffering he had been through? Nyapol knew pretty well that she had been very nasty at times too. But now she had apologized, he was quite prepared to start afresh. He remained quiet for a while enjoying the warmth of his wife's hands and thinking about what he would say. Before he opened his mouth, Nyilaji, the dying dog, barked for the first time in two weeks and rushed for the gate. Nyapol got up and followed it. She was terrified! Perhaps the dog had seen the shadow of the man Magungu had once seen. Ochola leaned out of bed to look. The children left off playing hide-and-seek and Abiero rushed out of the house. They all stared to see what was there. What could cause Nyilaji to jump up to bark and run when he was so near to death? Abiero overtook Nyapol as she reached the gate. He stood there motionless. Nyapol stared! She rubbed her eyes with the back of her hands and looked again! She was not dreaming! It was a visitor. Magungu had come back!

Magungu took the family by such surprise that nobody had the courage to greet him. He walked steadily towards them. When he was near he greeted them with the single word, "Peace". Tears glittered in Ochola's eyes when he heard the word. His saviour had come back to him! His hopes revived! He wished he had enough strength to leap to his feet and go to meet him. It was not only Ochola who regarded Magungu as the saviour, everybody did! Nyapol felt happier than she had been for weeks. Abiero heaved a sigh of relief. The tension of the last few weeks was released and the family felt as if a heavy shower had sponged away the oppressive heat of the afternoon.

First Magungu rested. Then after a wash, he sat down and talked to the family. He spoke about his journey and told them of the different places he had visited since he left them.

"Not once did I forget you," he added. "I couldn't get you out of my mind."

"We thought of you, too," the family replied in chorus.

Ochola's feeble voice continued alone, "I knew you would come back to us, son of Owuor. I felt it."

Then the family told Magungu about Ochola's admission to the white man's hospital at Pembe Tatu, and how he had come back home again with his condition unchanged. Magungu listened with keen interest.

"This is no illness for the white man's medicine," he commented.

Magungu carried Ochola back to the little hut which he had built to nurse him in, on his first visit.

At bed-time Magungu gave Ochola some sleeping medicine.

"Son of Owuor, remember — you told me you would come back with more powerful medicine," said Ochola. "I know this time I'll be completely cured. Soon I'll be leading a normal life. All this time I've been hoping and waiting. I knew you'd come back."

Ochola was asleep before he heard Magungu's reply.

That night Ochola dreamt that he was basking in the sun. Except for the children dancing nearby he was alone. Nyapol had gone to gather firewood. Abiero was out with the cattle. His mother came to see him. She brought oiled vegetables and millet flour steamed in milk. When he had eaten the food, his mother said, "Son, don't fear. You won't die in a foreign country. You'll soon go back to your own home and live amongst your own people again. You'll enjoy your inheritance, the land of our fathers. When your days in this world are completed, you will sleep amongst our people."

Before Ochola could reply or even ask his mother a question, he woke up.

183

Ochola lay for a long time, paralysed. The dream had frightened him. He must obey his mother. But even if he were to recover, he could not go back to Seme immediately. He would need another five or six years to amass the amount of wealth he had possessed before his illness. Only then could he fulfil his mother's wish and return to his birthplace. Ochola wanted to talk to some one about his dream. He wanted desperately to share it with his wife, but he was afraid. Nyapol wanted so much to return to Seme, and the fact that Ochola's mother had appeared to him in a dream would be a clear indication to her that they had to return at once. So Ochola kept quiet.

After breakfast Magungu told Ochola that he would try his new medicine on him. He did not waste time, but carried him outside and settled him under the *siala* tree, away from the family. He applied some oily medicine to Ochola's skin, working without speaking and ignoring all the questions Ochola asked him. When he had finished, Ochola was shivering all over, the pain had doubled and he felt that his whole body was being torn to pieces. Magungu asked him to try and bear it. He left his patient and went to call the family. He found them all waiting expectantly on the verandah of the house. Nyilaji, who was already improving, walked along with them to the place where Ochola was lying.

Then a miracle happened before their eyes. One by one the thorn-like warts started to fall out. They fell with such force and at such a speed that they looked like thin arrows being aimed at an enemy. The terrified family, who had come close to Ochola, started retreating as the arrow-like warts continued to fly in all directions. Nyapol clutched Abiero's coat like a frightened child and waited. When all the warts had fallen out, Magungu rubbed some herbs and ointment onto the open sores that were left. Soon the large holes from which the warts had come started to contract. Ochola's body began to look normal once more!

Nyapol looked on in wonder. This was the biggest miracle that she could ever witness. Ochola hardly believed that he had been healed. The fever and headache left him. His body felt free of pain for the first time for many months. A weary kind of smile radiated from his face when his eyes met those of the medicine-man. He looked at his arms; they were clean. He looked at his legs; they were clean! Then he ran his hands over his whole body; it was quite smooth. The God of his ancestors, the God of Magungu, the son of Owuor, had been merciful to him and healed him. He did not know how to show his gratitude. He stood up to see what it felt like to walk again, but his head felt light and he fell down at Magungu's feet. Nyapol stared at her husband, tears rolling fast down her cheeks. She wanted to take Ochola in her arms, yet she was afraid that Magungu's cure might not be permanent. She brought some porridge to her husband. Ochola ate, then slept.

Magungu called Nyapol and Abiero to his side. "My children," he said, "the God of mercy has blessed the son of Kisero and made him whole. But he'll only remain alive if he follows the voice of God. You must not sleep in this compound ever again, even tonight. You must leave for Seme at once, before the enemy has time to plant more medicine. Gather up the few things you can carry, and as soon as Ochola wakes up, you must go."

Nyapol looked at Abiero. Then her eyes moved quickly to Magungu. He must be mad. How could they start for

Seme as soon as Ochola woke up? The afternoon was already far gone. She had always longed to go back to Seme, but she had never imagined she would have to go in this way. What would she do with all the wealth that Ochola had accumulated? The granaries were full; the drums held beans and simsim. But that was not all! Ochola had a big kraal of cows, goats, and sheep, and a large chicken run. Abiero was dumbfounded.

Nyapol spoke to Magungu in a hoarse voice.

"Son of Owuor, my nerves are not strong nowadays, speak clearly. Why didn't you tell us yesterday that we should go home? Then I could have collected our things and bid 'good-bye' to our friends. We can't just leave like thieves in the night. What shall we do with all our wealth here?"

"You don't know what you are talking about, my child," Magungu said angrily. "The words of medicine are never known ahead. How could I have told you yesterday when I didn't know myself whether or not the medicine would work. Be grateful. Take the few things that you can carry, and be ready to leave when your husband wakes up. You have wept and prayed a thousand times for him to be cured. Now leave this home before another calamity befalls you. Wealth you can buy, but you cannot buy life. These are my final words!"

Nyapol went to the house to pack. She looked round at the wealth they had accumulated during the past three years and tears pricked her eyes. She did not know where to start; what should she take, and what should she leave? Her heart was drumming away as loudly as if she had been wrestling. She went into the bedroom, packed up some bedding and threw it into a small box. The blankets were so bulky that they filled the box, leaving no room for their clothes. She looked round for a larger box, but when Abiero appeared in the doorway, she ran to him.

"Abiero, Abiero, what have I done? Have I neglected the ancestors that they treat me so cruelly? What have we done, Abiero? Look at all these things! Look at all the cattle, sheep, goats and chickens! Look at all the bags of maize, millet and beans! Why must we lose everything and return to Seme empty-handed after all the suffering we have endured?" She sobbed loudly.

Abiero gripped Nyapol's shoulders tight.

"My sister, it's the will of God," he said. "We plan to go East, he turns our faces West. That my brother's wealth has to be left to the enemy tears my heart, but we have no choice, my sister, we must follow Magungu's advice."

The children were running up and down in the living-room.

Safari, the eldest son, clung to his mother's skirts, asking, "Mama, where are we going? Where are we going?"

"We're going home," Nyapol replied, weeping.

"But we are at home, Mama," Safari persisted.

"No, this is our second home, my son. We're going to our first home, in Seme. Now no more questions, Safari, the time is running short. Go and call Uncle to come and help me."

"But who will look after our house? Who will care for our cows and all our goats and our sheep and our chickens, Mama? I want to stay and look after my chickens, Mama. I'm going to stay!"

187

Seeing his mother was no longer listening to him, Safari ran and collected plates and cups from the shelves. He brought them and threw them all in the box where Nyapol was trying to fit in the bedding and clothes.

Then he stood aside and asked, "Can I bring some more, Mama?"

Nyapol looked at her son and forced a weak smile.

"No more, my son, we can't carry everything."

She wished she were a child once more, for during such desperate hours, a child's innocence carries him through.

Nyapol closed the box and then wrapped up a few more belongings in a cloth, which would be easier to carry. All the children had to be carried, and Ochola was still too weak to walk unsupported. Her hands trembled as she unlocked the little steel box where Ochola kept their money. She wrapped it up in her clothes.

Tired to death, Nyapol took the few belongings out into the yard. She changed her clothes and dressed the children. Then she told Magungu that she was ready. Abiero joined her with the few things he had collected. He was to carry the heaviest child, and he could not manage a large box as well. They were all standing in the middle of the compound waiting. Nyapol closed her eyes and her mind carried her back to Seme, the land of hills and valleys. She could see all her friends and relatives. She thought of the long sad months they had spent in this accursed village. Now they were to go away and leave it forever! She still felt that Magungu could have been more sensible and given them at least a week to sell their things. Then they could have arranged for a van to carry the remainder to the boat.

Ochola woke up very late. He looked around and saw the delicate evening sun. He thought it was early morning. Magungu was standing by him. Ochola had decided to give Magungu some cattle, several bags of food, and some money. Before Magungu returned to Kanyada, he would prepare a big feast to which he would invite all his friends. Everyone must meet the medicine-man who brought him back to life.

But Ochola's thoughts were interrupted.

Magungu called him, saying, "Ochola, Son of Kisero, listen to me. You're completely healed now. You are a normal man. Listen to the word of God. You should not sleep in this village again. You are going to Seme tonight. You must start this very minute. While you were sleeping I asked your wife and your brother to collect the few things they can carry on the journey. We must leave this haunted house before sunset. Look they are all ready! Here is some food. Eat quickly and let's be on our way. We'll travel all night and take the steamer across the lake in the morning."

Ochola thought he was dreaming. He pushed the food away and sat up. He lifted his eyes and looked round his compound. He saw cows in the stockade, and next to them, the goats and sheep. There were several stores of food, and in front of him stood the big house, full of expensive furniture. He had arrived at this place a poor man, almost a beggar. He had worked hard and become one of the wealthiest people in the land.

How could he go back to Seme empty-handed, poorer when he had left? If Magungu wanted him to leave, he then should at least have given him a few days to collect his property, sell what he could not carry, and obtain a licence to

189

move his cattle. Ah! Magungu could not be so heartless as to make him leave everything behind.

"I can't go," pleaded Ochola. "I must take my things with me. I can't go home empty-handed!"

He sat down on his bed again as if Magungu had not spoken to him.

"There is no time to waste," said Magungu, sternly. "The family is ready. Get up at once and let's go!"

Ochola got up, trembling. Sure enough, all the others were ready to leave. Nyapol, Abiero and the children were all waiting in the yard. The luggage was packed.

Ochola looked at his family with a broken heart. How could they listen to Magungu? How could they decide to leave without consulting him? Was he not the father of the family? Was he not the owner of the village? Ochola became wild with rage. He felt like a little child who had taken half a day moulding a clay bull, only to see it being trampled underfoot by an older boy.

He walked weakly towards his family, with his hands turned outwards.

"Nyapol, my dear," he cried. "How can you leave our beautiful house? Look at the fat cattle! Look at the sheep, the goats, the chickens and the food stores! Look at all these things that we've worked so hard to gain! How can we leave them all behind?"

Nyapol did not respond. She stood there with her head lowered. Then Ochola turned to Magungu, weeping unashamedly.

190

"Let me at least prepare a feast for my Luo friends so they may eat and enjoy all these riches before I go. Don't make me throw away all I have worked for. Let me have a party tonight — Okech will arrange it for me — then tomorrow we can go."

"No, Son of Seme," Magungu said furiously. "You've been healed when most people believed you would die. You should be thinking about your life, and the life of your wife and children. This isn't the time to arrange parties. If you stay alive, you have many years ahead for parties and for acquiring wealth. This village is doomed. You must not sleep here tonight."

Ochola broke away from Magungu's hand and started to run all over the compound like a mad man. When he looked back, Nyapol and Abiero were putting bundles on their heads, ready to leave. Ochola became wild with rage.

"Nyapol, what are you doing? How can you be so eager to go and leave everything behind? And where is my white cock? I can't leave my white cock behind."

He entered the house in a panic and saw his white cock in a corner. He caught and held it. Then he fumbled in the big wooden boxes, containing his clothes and some of the household goods, but instead of taking out what he wanted, he just rested his head on the boxes and wept.

"You are wasting our time, Ochola," Magungu called sternly from the doorway.

But Ochola did not hear him. He suddenly remembered his beloved dog. He almost let the white cock go free.

191

"Where is Nyilaji? Where is Nyilaji?" Ochola's heart started to beat even faster.

Why had he forgotten Nyilaji? He would leave everything behind, but he must take his dog, his brother, his friend. He ran out into the yard and called the dog as loudly as he could.

"Nyilaji — so, so, so, so."

Ochola hunted everywhere. When he went into the granary shed, he could hardly believe his eyes. Nyilaji was lying down, looking at him.

"What's wrong, Nyilaji?" he said to his dog. "Why didn't you come when I called you?"

Ochola reached out for the dog's collar, but it snapped at him and nearly bit off his fingers.

"What's wrong, my dog?" said Ochola, startled.

He threw down the cock without thinking and bent over to find out what was wrong with his dog. Magungu and Abiero who had followed, grabbed him by the shoulders and dragged him towards the gate.

"We must go! We must go! It's getting dark."

Ochola gathered all his strength and broke away from them and ran back to house. He had remembered some of his best photographs which were hanging on the wall. But the two powerful men took hold of him at the threshold of his house. This time they were determined not to allow him to escape.

"Let me just take my dog," he wept aloud. "Let me take Nyilaji home with me."

But the hard-hearted men would not listen. As they dragged him away, they passed Nyilaji, still squatting near the granary. Ochola made a last attempt to break loose and touch his dog, but they would not let him go.

At the gate Ochola stood firmly on the ground and looked round at his home. In the large enclosure, the cows called endlessly for their calves, their udders bursting with milk. The chickens were running hither and thither. The sheep and goats gathered near their hut, waiting for the door to be opened. The large granaries of maize, millet and beans stood there in the open space, bulging, like overfed children.

As Ochola gazed at his wonderful compound, Nyilaji ran towards him, stopped a few yards away, and howled. Once more Ochola pleaded with Magungu and Abiero.

"My brothers, look, my dog is close to me, let me take him home to comfort me now that I am losing all my possessions."

But the two men just shook their heads.

"Then let me touch him please! Let me say good-bye to him."

But they turned their heads and reminded him sternly, "We must leave here before the sun sinks below the earth."

The two men dragged him away. Darkness began to fall as they took the narrow path away from the compound.

Ochola's body was indeed going back to Seme. But his soul would stay forever in his home in Tanganyika.

They crossed the river and walked eastwards through the forest. As they walked, their ears could still catch the sounds emanating from the deserted compound. Nyilaji howled loudly, knowing now that he had been abandoned.

The noises died away slowly as the travellers wound their way through the forest. Ochola knew he would never forget his dog. He believed he would meet him in the next world.

*   *   *

Published by the East African Publishing House, Koinange Street, P. O. Box 30571 Nairobi and Printed in letterpress by East African Institute Press Ltd., Saldanha Lane, P. O. Box 30502, Nairobi, Kenya.